FRAME-UP ON THE BOWERY

By Tom Lalicki

FRAME-UP ON THE BOWERY

A HOUDINI & NATE MYSTERY

TOM LALICKI

Pictures by **Carlyn Beccia**

FARRAR STRAUS GIROUX
NEW YORK

*For Florence and Bill Hasbrouck, always steady
and cautiously optimistic—a winning combination*

Text copyright © 2009 by Tom Lalicki
Pictures copyright © 2009 by Carlyn Beccia
All rights reserved
Distributed in Canada by Douglas & McIntyre Ltd.
Printed in July 2009 in the United States of America
by RR Donnelley, Harrisonburg, Virginia
Designed by Jay Colvin
First edition, 2009

1   3   5   7   9   10   8   6   4   2

www.fsgkidsbooks.com

Library of Congress Cataloging-in-Publication Data

Lalicki, Tom.
    Frame-up on the Bowery : a Houdini & Nate mystery / Tom Lalicki ; pictures by
Carlyn Beccia.— 1st ed.
        p.   cm.
    Summary: Thirteen-year-old Nate, aided by his newly discovered cousin and the
famous magician Harry Houdini, catches the Fifth Avenue Slasher, solves a string of
burglaries, and stops a notorious gang leader.
    ISBN: 978-0-374-39930-6
    1. Houdini, Harry, 1874–1926—Juvenile fiction.   [1. Houdini, Harry, 1874–1926—
Fiction.   2. Magicians—Fiction.   3. Cousins—Fiction.   4. Mystery and detective
stories.]   I. Beccia, Carlyn, ill.   II. Title.

PZ7.L1594Fr 2009
[Fic]—dc22

                                                                    2008045607

FRAME-UP ON THE BOWERY

Crime is naught but misdirected energy.
—Emma Goldman, activist

Prologue

Hearing the scream, Nate flew down the back stairs and dashed into the kitchen, expecting to find Marina bleeding uncontrollably. Or on the floor with a broken bone sticking out of her skin. Something ghastly and life-threatening.

Instead, the cook sat in a chair near the stove, where she sighed and sobbed, pressing a copy of the *New York World* to her chest. Marina's daughter, Beatrycze the maid, gestured at the newspaper page. Mother and daughter had recently immigrated from Poland and spoke little English.

"Murder!" Marina sobbed deeply. "Murder *next block*. Grocer boy told me it is in this paper."

"Ya, ya! Grocer delivery boy said *murder*," Bea agreed, making it sound like *moor-dur*.

Nate took the paper and smoothed out the wrinkles on the surface of the kitchen table.

"New York, December sixteenth, 1911," he began, and read the headlines with growing dread:

BRUTAL MURDER ON EAST 54TH STREET
PROMINENT STOCKBROKER
TORTURED AND MUTILATED
NO SUSPECTS IN DEMONIC CRIME

"One block away? Is true? *One block?*" Marina asked feverishly.

"Let me read the story and then I'll tell you all about it," Nate said, trying to reassure her.

But it was a grisly story. Frightening.

A criminal the newspaper dubbed the "Fifth Avenue Slasher" had killed Carl Templeton Cramer, a stockbroker. The murder happened in Cramer's splendid home on East Fifty-fourth street and Fifth Avenue—only a block away.

That explained why the grocer's delivery boy had thoroughly frightened the servants. He probably felt like he was doing a public service, while picking up a few extra pennies, by selling copies of the newspaper to unlikely customers such as cooks and maids.

The *New York World*'s story went on to say that the victim had returned home unexpectedly, having left the Astors' Christmas ball early. Police assumed that Cramer stepped into his library and discovered a thief ransacking the room. The burglar bashed his head in—probably with a statuette taken in the robbery—and tied him up. The villain then tortured Cramer, dragging a sharp knife across his face and neck dozens of times, presumably to get the combination to his safe. When called to the scene, police found the safe open—and emptied.

The story became more frenzied and fear-provoking at this point:

> His bloodlust satisfied at long last, the fiend inflicted his coup de grâce—a slash from one side of the neck to the other. Mercifully, death followed swiftly.
>
> Police at the scene determined that the victim's person had been robbed of watch, rings, tiepin, billfold, and even his cigars. "Cool as a cucumber this Slasher was," a detective lieutenant told this reporter. "Put all his swag in a satchel, I'd guess, and went to the kitchen, unbolted the door, and walked away free as a bird." This reporter saw bloody footprints—made in the blood of his innocent victim—that confirm the Fifth Avenue Slasher's unhurried mode of egress.

"One of our city's most successful, personable, and charitable citizens, Carl Templeton Cramer will be sorely missed," the paper's reporter added in an editorial.

In an adjoining story, the *World* wondered whether the criminal responsible for a number of recent but nonviolent burglaries that had taken place in Nate's neighborhood had turned into a bloodthirsty maniac.

If that theory was true, no homeowner was safe. Nate peeked over the top of the paper at the cowering women. *They don't need to hear this part of it.*

The detective lieutenant had no comment on the *World*'s speculation, but assured the public that everything humanly possible would be done to find the Fifth Avenue Slasher.

Nate lowered the paper, took a deep breath, and summarized the story for Marina and Bea in the least frightening words he could find. Privately, he guessed many people in the neighborhood would sleep uneasily until the police made an arrest.

1

The Christmas holiday was shaping up as the worst Nate could remember. He had piles of schoolwork to do before January. Worse, he couldn't even take a break to dash uptown and visit Houdini.

Of course, I can't remember ever having a bad Christmas before, Nate told himself. *When I visit Ace tomorrow, maybe Houdini will drop in to his workshop and say hello. Regardless, just look at all the things I'm learning, like the furnace man's name.*

Before yesterday, Nate had never thought about furnace men. Every home in New York employed these coal stokers, but their calls weren't social events. Furnace men went silently from house to house every winter night.

They let themselves in through a cellar door, tended the coal fire, and left. If they didn't, the fire would go out overnight, leaving a house without heat or hot water.

Normally Marina or Bea would leave the cellar door open until the stoker had finished his work and banged the pipes to signal that he was leaving. Then they would lock up. But yesterday they both came down with the same flu that had sent Nate's mother and Aunt Alice to their beds. Too sick to stay up, the cook and maid buttoned up all the doors, drew the curtains, and took to their beds on the top floor. Luckily Nate heard Joe the furnace man's incessant banging and let him in.

"Smart thinking locking up," Joe had said after introducing himself. "You're not safe in your own house these days . . . with that Slasher on the loose."

Nate nodded agreement. Five days had passed, but the search for the Fifth Avenue Slasher was still the main story—practically the *only* story—in a half dozen newspapers. The police had a hundred men working on the case and promised that an arrest was pending. But a pending arrest didn't make people feel safe under their covers; bolted doors did.

"It's Old Sparky the electric chair for that one," Joe observed when Nate let him in this evening.

"A cold-blooded murder . . . the victim slowly tortured," Nate recited from the article. "Juries show no mercy to killers who show none themselves," he added, drawing from the extensive reading about crime and

8

criminals he'd done since meeting his friend and mentor, Harry Houdini.

Nate had met Houdini by chance—he was a customer of the hat store where Nate had worked the previous summer. Good thing, too. Otherwise the phony medium who had Aunt Alice totally conned would have taken her house, her money, and probably her life.

After letting the soot-covered furnace man out for a second evening, Nate bolted the cellar door and went halfway up the stairs before returning to test the bolt. Then he smiled at himself and went upstairs.

He was tired. Nursing all these ailing women in a four-story brownstone was no easy job. He had run up and down more flights of stairs that day than he could believe. Now that everyone was sleeping, Nate happily dropped onto the sofa and back into his studies.

We could all have frozen to death last night if I hadn't heard Joe's banging.

Well, we'd have been very cold, he corrected himself, trying not to exaggerate. Houdini had once said, "Exaggeration is the essence of publicity—but the archenemy of observation and deduction."

"Very cold" was no exaggeration. The weather was unbearably cold and windy for December. It made him shiver to think of being outside.

Casting an eye halfheartedly back to the task at hand—algebra problems—Nate felt his mood darkening. He was good at every other subject. He even liked most of

them. But now that he was frantically trying to make up for a lost semester, math was an even bigger problem than usual.

Within seconds, his mind drifted. The mysterious symbols and numbers turned into tiny insects scurrying across the paper. Unconsciously Nate scratched himself—first his wrist, then his leg, then his ankles—without relief. A woolen union suit—toe-to-neck, one-piece underwear—attacked his skin like an army of ants. The itch danced about his body more quickly than his hands could follow.

Raps at the front door brought him to his senses. Putting the algebra aside, Nate rushed to the entrance hall.

"Can I help you?" he asked a young girl shivering on the stoop.

"Why yes, you surely can," she replied in the unmistakable drawl of a Southerner. "Is this the home of Mrs. Alice Ludlow?"

"It is," he said, and hesitated. The girl had a frayed cotton shawl wrapped around her throat and nothing more than a canvas jacket to protect her from the piercing wind.

"Are you delivering something?"

"No, not as like . . ."

Nate was stumped. The girl had none of the swagger of a New York City street urchin. And she clearly wasn't the child of one of Aunt Alice's friends. During an uncomfortable silence, Nate deduced that she had arrived in a han-

som cab waiting in the street. He saw the outline of an adult passenger in the cab's rear compartment.

"Is that your cab? Are you with the person in that cab?" Nate asked, pointing at the horse-drawn carriage.

"I rightly am," she proclaimed proudly. "That's my *pa* in the cab."

"Well . . ." Nate said, considering the unusual situation, "does your father wish to see Mrs. Ludlow? Is your father a friend, a business connection?"

"My pa has urgent business elsewhere. He has no time to visit, and came only to see that I am properly situated," the girl said stiffly, as if reciting a memorized speech.

Nate broke out laughing; he had never heard the word *situated* pronounced *sitch-e-ate-ed* before.

"Jerusalem Crickets! Is that how you treat Aunt Alice's kin up here? You horse-laugh at them?"

"Excuse me," Nate said, bowled over by the tiny creature's fit of temper. Her back had stiffened; there was flint in her voice. "Kin? You're related to my aunt Alice?"

"*Your* aunt Alice!" she said excitedly, her mood changing yet again. "You must be Cousin Nate." The child rushed forward, threw her arms around Nate's waist, and squeezed tightly.

A heartbeat later, Nate saw a disembodied arm hurl a carpetbag onto the pavement from the back of the hansom cab. Then, without a word or a wave, the cab took off toward Fifth Avenue.

2

The girl all but disappeared inside the quilt Nate had wrapped around her. She had collapsed on the sofa, shivering, her teeth chattering. Nate let her warm up thoroughly, and drink two generous mugs of cocoa, before even asking her name.

"Allie. Course, Alice is my Christian name, but nobody ever calls me anything 'cept Allie."

"You were named after my aunt Alice?"

"That's what Pa says: 'I named you after my sister 'cause I saw at first sight you were gonna be an ornery, cussed little mite,'" Allie recalled fondly, then added briskly, "and she's *my* aunt, too."

"Your father is Aunt Alice's brother . . . I've never, ever heard Aunt Alice talk about a brother."

"Bad blood," she said slowly, shaking her head from side to side. "Cuz, this chocolate is awful fine, but do you think I could rustle up some real food in the kitchen?"

"Certainly . . . I should have offered . . ."

"Don't fret. You're the most helpful man about the kitchen I ever met," she said, throwing aside the quilt and dashing toward the hall. "Let's see what I can cook up for the two of us."

Nate caught up with her in front of the icebox, where she stood mesmerized by the food before her.

"Godfrey Daniel! Ham. And eggs. Milk!" She turned to Nate in wonder and said, "I bet none of it is salted or sour."

"Well, that's the point of an icebox, isn't it?" Nate asked uncertainly. "The ice keeps the food fresh."

"I know that, silly. I've *seen* iceboxes before. I just never had one."

Nate nodded noncommittally.

"I'm not a cook," he said. "I'd ask Marina to make something, but—"

"Who's Marina?"

"Our cook."

"Mother of Pearl! Pa said you folk live like kings, but I thought he was jokin' me," Allie said. "A cook."

"Speaking of your *father*, when—"

"He's your uncle Jack. Great-uncle Jack Skinner," she clarified.

"Thank you. When do you expect Uncle Jack to join us?"

Allie giggled and smiled privately; Nate pressed her. "Later this evening? I'm sure Aunt Alice will be interested."

Now Allie laughed out loud.

"Not before spring, child," she said seriously, imitating a man's voice. " 'Not before spring, child' is what he told me before I got out of that horse cart that brought us here."

"And what did you say to that?" an astonished Nate asked.

" 'Spring of what year?' That's what I said to him: 'Spring of what year?' " she said with tremendous satisfaction. Nate wondered if she had truly been abandoned on the doorstep.

"You mind if I make some bacon and eggs?" she said while putting ingredients on the counter near the stove. Nate assisted, mechanically, as if in a trance. He passed her a heavy frying pan, a spatula, butter—if they had lard, he had no idea where it was. He sliced some bread, and she devoured a piece before he could suggest toasting it. The child was ravenous but happy as a songbird. She hummed with a full mouth and prepared a meal as if she had been born in a kitchen. Nate stepped aside and leaned against the far wall.

Every situation is a one-of-a-kind, Houdini had told him. *Enjoy! But analyze, always analyze before you act. Because instinct usually puts you "in a stink."*

Allie wore a knee-length dress of very light cotton. It was a green and red plaid with a patch in plain green fabric. Her hay-colored hair was tied in a pigtail with a pink ribbon. Her black socks showed numerous repairs. He doubted that the banged-up carpetbag she'd fetched from the street held any newer garb.

She was small and poorly dressed, but Nate recognized that she was quite a character. Allie would be ten in three weeks, she'd told him earlier. That made her the first relative close to his own age that Nate had seen since his mother's Connecticut brothers had packed their families off to Michigan.

If she is my cousin . . . how . . . why would Aunt Alice keep something like that a secret?

"Introduce me to our guest, please," Nate's mother said hoarsely, interrupting his speculations about family secrets. She held the doorframe unsteadily, a shawl wrapped around her robe.

"You shouldn't be out of bed," Nate said as he helped her to a chair.

"Are you Nate's mother?" Allie yelled from the stove. "I am sooooo glad to meet you."

Nate looked at his mother. "Mrs. Deborah Fuller, let me introduce you to Alice Skinner, the daughter of Jack Skinner. My cousin," he added, half questioning.

Nate's mother stared at Allie and brightened. "You are Jack Skinner's *daughter*? I had no idea Jack had a child."

"I'm her, in the pink," Allie said.

"I had no idea there was a Jack Skinner in the family," Nate said.

"Of course you didn't, Nate. I've never met him. Your father mentioned him before we were married. And that was only to caution me never to mention Jack Skinner to Aunt Alice."

"Bad blood!" Allie repeated with her theatrical head wagging.

"Well, that bad blood doesn't apply to me," Deborah Fuller said, "and I am thrilled to make your acquaintance, Alice. I would hug you, but don't dare for fear of giving you this horrible flu."

"I ain't scared," she said, rushing to embrace Nate's mother, "and it's just Allie."

Deborah Fuller shook and coughed, but Allie clung tightly to her.

"The thing is, Mother, that Allie doesn't expect to see her father for quite some time," Nate said.

"Not before spring," Allie said gruffly, her voice muffled by Deborah Fuller's robe.

"Excuse me?"

Nate shrugged his shoulders uncertainly.

"Allie, have you come to live with us?" Nate's mother asked. The child buried her head more deeply into Deborah Fuller's lap before saying, "My pa said he had important business in California. Said he was gonna make a fortune but couldn't do it if I slowed him down."

"That's terrible," Nate's mother said, and instantly regretted saying it.

"But it's true. I'm little . . . and I'm slow compared to my pa. And makin' money is for men."

Allie unclenched and stepped back from Nate's mother. "Besides, my pa said I need some women in my life—to 'civilize me,' he said. He always promised that someday he'd bring me to meet you."

"Is Aunt Alice expecting you?" Nate asked.

"There wasn't rightly time to tell her," Allie said. "One night last week Pa came through the door and said, 'Child, Georgia's not the place for us anymore. You pack—and be quick about it.' You can bet I was. And now I'm here."

"And your father?" Deborah Fuller asked.

"He's probably halfway to California," Allie said with a smile.

Right then, Nate discovered something. He had finally found something more mysterious than algebra—families.

3

I thought I'd seen it all yesterday," Nate said, marveling at the sight of Allie being bundled up in his Christmas church-going coat and his gloves and school cap—all far too big for her. "But it just keeps getting better."

Reluctantly Nate had agreed that his cousin could accompany him on his visit to Houdini's workshop, where his friend Ace worked.

"I didn't ask to wear your stuff. My things are just fine, Cousin Deborah."

"Hush! Both of you," commanded Nate's mother. She was still quite ill, but had found remarkable reservoirs of vitality since Allie had walked into their lives the previous afternoon.

Aunt Alice had no idea that a niece she had never before laid eyes on was being hidden in her own house. Nate's mother had insisted that they weren't hiding their unexpected guest.

"Aunt Alice is far too ill to appreciate meeting you, my dear," she had told Allie. "Tomorrow—when your aunt is stronger."

And Allie had good-naturedly gone along with the deception. She and Nate ate dinner together in the kitchen, after which Allie helped prepare soup and tea for all the invalids. And while Nate spent an hour reading a *Ladies' Home Journal* Christmas story to his drowsy great-aunt, Allie cleaned the kitchen *and* dusted the parlor.

Then, at Deborah Fuller's insistence, Allie was whisked quietly up the servants' back stairway to the top floor, where Nate tucked her away in one of the servants' rooms, careful not to awaken the cook or her daughter.

It wasn't just that Nate didn't want Allie tagging along. After all, he hadn't seen Ace in months. He had never seen Houdini's workshop before. And it wasn't entirely out of the question that Houdini would come downstairs to visit himself, once he heard that Nate was there.

"But *how* do I explain Allie?" Nate asked his mother after Allie was asleep. "She's a cousin I never met until yesterday, when her father threw her clothes into the street and took off in a cab."

"It won't be a problem, Nate," his mother insisted. "After all, Ace was abandoned by his father, wasn't he?"

"That's true."

"On the other hand, I have no idea how Alice will react to this situation. It's better if I tell her when we are alone," she said, coughing viciously.

So Nate had agreed to bring his cousin because he couldn't deny his mother's reasonable request. Nate's mother wrapped a silk scarf around Allie's neck as final protection against the bitter cold, and they were off to 278 West 113th Street—the Houdini homequarters.

Allie was too overwhelmed by the sights and sounds of New York City to say a word until they exited the subway at 110th Street.

"So many people . . . I bet I seen more people this morning than there are in the whole state of Georgia. And they're all in such a hurry, like to knock you over."

"You'll get used to it," Nate said, "if you stay here, that is."

"And that subway . . . Godfrey Daniel! A whole railroad train that runs under the ground."

"Get ready to *really* be amazed. Here is the Houdinis'," Nate said, pressing a buzzer at the brownstone's special basement entrance. Seconds later, a voice called out, "Fuller, is that you?"

"You bet it is, Ace," Nate replied eagerly.

"All right," Ace said as the sound of chains being dragged over metal pulleys commenced. Slowly, the huge rectangular door began to slide open.

"Houdini had this door put in so we could get equipment in and out," Ace yelled, "but I think it's big enough to drive a bus through."

The noise stopped when the door was about one-third opened and Ace came bounding out.

"Nathaniel Green Makeworthy Fuller the Fourth, as I live and breathe. Put it there, buddy," he said, extending a hand. At sixteen, Ace Winchell was considerably taller than Nate. Judging by his grip, he was considerably stronger, too.

"I guess working for Houdini is tougher than being a salesclerk," Nate said, referring to the summer job where he had met Ace.

Nate considered himself forever in debt to Ace for the part his pal had played in cracking the phony medium caper, and for saving Nate's life along the way.

"It's better every way you can imagine, let me tell you. Hey, who's the kid there? Is she with you?"

"Pleased to meet you," she said, stepping forward. "Allie Skinner's my name."

"I didn't say you could bring no kids from the neighborhood," Ace said rather sharply. "Mrs. Houdini said it was okay for you to see the workshop, but I can't let no strangers in."

Nate dragged Ace aside and filled him in on his emerging family situation. Ace walked back and stood in front of Allie, eyeing her suspiciously. Finally he ordered them both to stand outside until he returned.

"He sure is a grouch," Allie said.

"Not in the least," Nate insisted. "Everyone who works for Houdini swears a solemn oath to protect Houdini's secrets, to never, *ever* give them up. For all Ace knows, you could be a spy."

"Go on now."

"Says you . . . I've only got your word that we're related."

"But that's plain—"

"Be still," Nate said, seeing Ace at the door.

"All right, come in. I put the plans away."

Nate intended to ask "what plans" but was so astonished by his first look inside Houdini's legendary magic workshop that he was utterly speechless. Not so Allie.

"What a whole lot of junk!" she exclaimed.

4

Junk!" Ace repeated in utter disbelief. "I should bounce you out of here right on your ear, talking that way."

"She didn't mean anything, Ace. She just doesn't have any idea what she's looking at—she's from the country." Nate dropped his voice to a confidential whisper. "Tell us, what *are* we looking at?"

Ace glowered at Allie for a few seconds before clearing his throat.

"Well then, all right. What we have in all these packing cases is equipment for Houdini's act. These two have his Milk Can and backup Milk Can. You can see they're securely locked and chained—there's dozens of cheaters who would pay a fortune to get hold of one of those cans."

"Nate, are milk cans really so valuable?" Allie asked innocently.

"See what I mean?" Nate scoffed, encouraging Ace to continue.

He did, pointing out dozens of magic props scattered among an amazing array of objects, from chains and padlocks hanging from wall hooks and animal and bird cages to human torso and head figures and dress forms in three different sizes.

"Is *that* what I think it is?" Nate asked, pointing toward a partially covered piece of furniture.

Ace smiled broadly. "If you think it's Sparky Number One, New York's first electrocution chair, you're dead-on. Pun intended."

Nate cautiously walked nearer. The plain pine chair had rough leather restraints attached to its armrests and legs. Nate sat down.

"I'll do you up," volunteered Ace. "They retired this chair for a new one and Houdini bought it for fun. Every time he puts it in his office, Mrs. Houdini calls and tells me to bring it back here."

In no time at all, Nate's arms and legs were tied to the chair. Ace then pulled a leather belt around his chest and cinched it as tight as possible, but still it was loose.

"I guess they never fried anybody your size at Sing Sing," Ace joked, referring to the big state prison north of New York City.

"Nate, I don't like this," Allie said. "Please get out of that machine."

"Oh, for pity's sake, there's nothing to be scared of," Nate replied.

"That's right, nothing at all," Ace said, "even though I'm putting the skullcap that carries the juice on your noggin."

The cap, made of iron bands, covered Nate's eyes rather than sitting on his forehead.

"The juice wire is still attached to the cap," Ace said. "If I throw that switch on the wall," he said with all the menace possible, "your hair will catch fire first. Then your brain will cook—like beef on a grill. What do you say we try it?"

But as Ace took a step toward the imaginary wall switch, Allie dove at him, throwing furious punches at his midsection.

"You leave my cousin alone, you low-down rat!" she cried.

"Stop, Allie! It's a joke," Nate said, trying not to laugh. Ace got Allie by her shoulders and restrained the swinging, squirming girl.

"This one's got a lot of spunk, Fuller. Not long on brains though."

Realizing her error, Allie stopped struggling, and Ace let go. She found a wooden crate, sat noisily, and proceeded to sulk. Nate and Ace ignored her.

"What did you have to hide earlier? Before we could enter?"

"The blueprints for Houdini's Water Torture Escape," Ace whispered.

"I couldn't care less what you're all talking about," Allie said loudly.

"A new escape? As good as the Milk Can?" Nate asked.

"Better. We're making the best escape Houdini ever did."

"Wow, I had no idea you were working on it," Nate said, regretting that he was home struggling with algebra while Ace was here collaborating with Houdini.

"Well, right now I'm just learning the ropes. I'm the builder's assistant. But he helps design Houdini's props, too. So someday I'll take his job—designing and building them, going on the road and keeping the act running smooth. Right now, I'll admit my most important jobs are cleaning up, helping out Mrs. Houdini's friends, and walking Charlie."

"Where is Charlie?" Nate asked at the mention of Houdini's beloved pet.

"Mrs. Houdini took him Christmas shopping today."

"Just the two of them?"

"Yeah. Houdini's in his library, most likely. He is every day that he doesn't go out to the cemetery to visit his mother's grave."

Nate bowed his head respectfully.

"If Houdini doesn't snap out of it, I don't know if we'll *ever* get this water torture prop built. Mrs. Houdini is losing hope, I think," Ace continued unhappily. "She gave my boss the month off. I'm here mostly so she'll have some-body to talk to, if you ask me."

"Can you show me the prop?" Nate asked, purposely changing the subject. "Houdini had me take his secrecy oath, you know. So I can see anything."

"Yeah, but . . ." Ace said, and flicked his thumb at Allie.

"I'll just turn around and close my eyes so you *boys* can look at your secret *things*," she said.

Ace stroked his chin thoughtfully. "It's safe enough for you to look at it, Fuller, and I don't think she could figure out how to work a doorknob."

"Sticks and stones can break my bones, but—"

"We know how it goes, Allie. And he's only joking with you," Nate said as he followed Ace past trunks stacked to his right. Scanning them, Nate couldn't guess which ones were part of Houdini's escape act and which were simply luggage. On the left wall were a half dozen evil-looking straitjackets. Made of leather and canvas, each had gro-tesquely long sleeves to incapacitate mental patients by cinching their arms across their bodies. Houdini escaped from them while hanging upside down from skycrapers. *Incredible,* Nate thought, fingering one of them. Peeking backward, he saw Allie edging her way behind them.

"What's that?" Nate asked, pointing to a frightening iron chair studded with sharpened spikes and leather restraints.

"That's a Witch's Chair. It came from some old prison. I heard it took the boss over an hour to escape from it. He liked it so much he brought it home, I guess."

Ace stopped next to a large rectangular object. Completely covered by a canvas tarpaulin, it was at least five feet high and two feet wide.

"Behold!" Ace said, pulling the tarp away with a flourish. He had uncovered a tall glass container held together by highly polished mahogany pillars. Close up, Nate realized that the glass walls were nearly an inch thick.

"Houdini will escape from this?" he asked.

"It's really going to be something," Ace said proudly. He picked up a rectangular piece of wood and held it out.

"This is the lid, see. First Houdini is handcuffed. Then he'll put his feet through these holes in the lid." Ace demonstrated by stepping into the wooden frame. "Then chains are attached to these hooks and a winch pulls Houdini into the air feetfirst. Then he's lowered into the glass cabinet here, four padlocks lock the cabinet, and it's covered up. Then Houdini has to escape."

"So he's upside down in a glass box?" Allie said, standing with her back to them. "So what?"

"I think you left something out," Nate suggested.

"Oh, right . . . You see, kid, after Houdini gets locked upside down in the cabinet, it's filled with over a hundred gallons of water," Ace said.

"Getting out of handcuffs and leg shackles upside down isn't much of a challenge for Houdini," Nate said sincerely. "Doing it before he drowns is the challenge."

Allie turned around and walked toward the case fascinated.

"You mean he's upside down, underwater, and his feet are outside the glass box? And the lock is outside. And he's handcuffed to start? Shucks, how long can he stay underwater?"

"He hopes to escape in less than five minutes," Ace said.

"He better do it a lot quicker, 'cause nobody could hold their breath underwater that long," she said firmly.

"You don't know Houdini," Nate replied with a smile.

"Well, wouldn't that beat all? If he could do it and live, I'd sure like to meet this Houdini. He sounds a lot like my pa."

"Your father has the disappearing down pat. He would have to reappear before I compare him to Houdini," Nate joked, sparking a spirited rebuttal from Allie.

But seeing Houdini wasn't in the cards for that day. Ace swore that he had told Houdini Nate was coming, but the workshop door never opened from the kitchen above. And Ace had no intention of interrupting his boss, not even for Nate.

"He probably forgot to mark it in his calendar," Nate told Allie. "Another time."

The group spent a full hour exploring the workshop before lunching at a neighborhood drugstore. When they parted, Allie and Ace were the best of friends.

5

"They are wanting you upstairs," Bea the maid said foggily as Nate and Allie opened the front door. She looked ghastly—pale and splotchy red simultaneously. "I go back to bed now, yes?"

"Definitely," Nate said. After hanging his winter things on pegs, Nate turned to help Allie. There was no need. She piled everything in Nate's arms and raced to the stairs, saying, "I am so looking forward to meeting Aunt Alice finally."

Nate caught up to her just as she rushed toward the open doorway of the master bedroom.

"Stop! Stand still! Let me see what you're made of." Aunt Alice's orders froze Allie in midflight, a leg in the air.

The elderly woman squinted at the girl from her bed, at the foot of which perched Nate's mother, smiling at the rigid—and terrified—Allie. Aunt Alice flapped a hand to indicate that the girl could lower her airborne limb.

"Can I come in and say hello, Aunt Alice?" Allie asked.

Aunt Alice waved her in, and Nate followed.

"Is it possible, Deborah? Has the world become so depraved? Parents simply abandon children?" she asked, staring at Allie without making eye contact.

"I think that's too harsh, Alice. Surely he will return," Deborah Fuller said.

"Only he? There is no mother involved?"

"If you mean my ma, she passed a long, *long* time ago, Aunt Alice. You never met her, my pa says."

Aunt Alice's hand shook noticeably as she asked, "Do you know your mother's name, child?"

"Course I do. Before she married, Ma's name was Clarisse Geronde."

Aunt Alice lowered her eyeglasses and slumped backward. Nate thought she said "Cursed!" under her breath.

"Years ago, long after my own dear mother's death, my father married a charming young woman. Her name was Louisa Geronde," Aunt Alice recalled, looking at the ceiling. "Louisa was from New Orleans. She was young enough to be my sister, and we got along like sisters."

"Was she kin to my ma?"

"It is probable," Aunt Alice said sharply. "Gerondes are *plentiful* in Louisiana."

They were silent until Aunt Alice told Allie to sit in a chair against the far wall. Then she continued her story. Allie, back straight as a rod, sat listening with dreamy eyes, as if to a bedtime story.

"It seemed as if Jack had his opinions from the day he learned to speak. Jack and my father never saw eye to eye. As Jack grew older, the quarrels grew more bitter."

"Fathers and sons always tangle with each other," Nate's mother put in.

"Not like they did. Eventually, Father told Jack to live by his rules or leave. Jack left. Father was furious. Disinherited him—his own son," Aunt Alice said tearfully. "Jack tried to mend fences a few years later, but Father wouldn't let Jack near the house—wouldn't read Jack's letters or let me read them to him."

"But when your father died, *you* could have made up," Nate said.

"I wanted to. I would have, but by then Jack had disappeared—without a trace."

"I guess that he went to Georgia," Nate said. "Allie came from there."

"I was born in *New Orleans*. And there'll always be a place for me at Belltaire, that's what my granny wrote last Christmas."

"Belltaire?" Aunt Alice asked. "Do you also know a house called Chalfont?"

"I sure do. Pa said that was where his ma was born, but

we could never go inside because some Yankees stole it from us."

"Northerners stole your mother's house? Really?" Nate asked skeptically.

"Well, Pa meant that they bought it real cheap . . . He meant they might as well have stolen it," Allie explained.

"Marrying his own mother's cousin . . . your father is a most unreliable man, child," Aunt Alice said.

"Sometimes Pa gets confused. And he says things that don't work out right. But he's reliable as the sunrise," Allie said.

"Then where is he now?" Aunt Alice challenged.

"Making our fortune. He'll be back by spring with a pile of money. He promised."

The telephone rang in the hallway below. Knowing Marina and Bea were in bed on the floor above, Nate listened closely to the ring sequence, in case the call was for them.

Two long rings, one short, and another long—it was for Nate's family, not one of the others that shared their party line.

"I should get it," he said, wishing he could do a Houdini and be in two places at the same time. He sprinted for the stairs.

"Hello, this is Longacre 6533," he said loudly into the speaker fixed to the wall. He pressed the black candlestick-shaped receiver to his ear and listened for a reply.

"Nate, is this you? I hope that I am not disturbing the wrong person," a familiar woman's voice said.

"Mrs. Houdini? This is Nate."

"Nate, is it a convenient time to speak?" she asked. "Ach, where are my manners? How are your mother and great-aunt?"

"Not their best—the flu, you know," Nate answered.

"Is your cook giving them chicken broth? That's the best."

"Cook is sick, too. And her daughter. But we're doing well enough."

"It is not a good time to bother you then . . . But it is urgent," Mrs. Houdini said.

"What's wrong, Mrs. Houdini?"

"I am calling about Leslie."

"Ace?"

"Yes, the boy you call Ace."

"I just left him at Kruger's Drug Store—no more than two hours ago. What's wrong with him?" Nate asked.

"He is in trouble," Mrs. Houdini said gravely. "Terrible trouble!"

"What sort of trouble?" Nate asked.

"The prison sort . . ."

"Prison?"

Mrs. Houdini plunged into a tide of impassioned German. It was the language she spoke growing up, and Nate didn't comprehend a word of it.

"I'm sorry. I can't understand you."

"It is . . . what do I mean . . . a nightmare! Leslie was taken to jail. He was outside helping my neighbor Mr. Bonamino with his automobile when *two* police wagons came."

"Are you sure they arrested him?" Nate asked.

"Mr. Bonamino was. He said policemen surrounded Leslie with guns drawn. They handcuffed the dear boy, pushed him in a car, and sped away."

"What did he do?" Nate exclaimed. "I mean, what do they *say* he did?" he corrected himself quickly. Ace knew a lot of criminals; he made no bones about it. But that didn't make Ace a criminal himself, any more than working for Houdini made him an escape artist.

"I do not know."

"Did your neighbor ask them?"

"He asked, of course, but the policemen would not tell him," Mrs. Houdini said, growing breathless. She paused to collect herself and went on, "I know it is a serious charge, Captain Root told me that."

"Captain Root arrested Ace?"

The captain was a good friend of the Houdinis, now assigned to the new Police Headquarters on Centre Street. He had once thought Ace was just another street hooligan; surely Ace's helping to foil the phony medium had changed his opinion. Nate wondered why he of all people would come to arrest Ace.

"No. I called him. He seemed to know very much, but did not like telling me over the telephone."

"What does Houdini think?" Nate asked.

"I did not wish to disturb Houdini . . . that is why *I* called the captain. He is coming here . . . to 278. You will come?"

"I will hop the subway and—"

"But the captain is waiting to hear if he should pick you up in his police car. If that is convenient," added Mrs. Houdini.

Convenient. Is there ever a convenient time for bad things to happen?

"If you think I can help, count me in, Mrs. Houdini. Tell the captain I will be waiting," Nate said. Returning the receiver to its brass hook, he looked upward and readied himself to tell his mother and Aunt Alice that he was going to the Houdinis'—and had no idea when he would return.

6

It took some explaining, but the fact that Mrs. Houdini had requested his presence appeased Aunt Alice, who recalled that "she is a most agreeable acquaintance; excellent manners." And the fact that Captain Root was driving satisfied Nate's mother that "it must be some important matter."

Only Allie was unhappy—because she wanted to go, too.

"Sorry, but not this time," Nate said as he went to his room to fetch pencils and paper. He liked to keep case notes, a written record of interviews, observations, and hypotheses, just as professional detectives did. As he rummaged around on his desk, his glance was forcibly pulled to the scrapbook he kept at one side. The massive leather book—handsomely monogrammed NATHANIEL GREEN MAKEWORTHY FULLER in ornate gold lettering—was a present from Mrs. Houdini. It had arrived the day after the Houdinis returned from Europe, with a note:

> My dearest Nate,
> I hope that you do not mind too much my recording the beginning of your famous career.
>
> > Most fondly,
> > Bess Houdini

"I'll say I don't mind!" Nate had exclaimed to his mother when he looked inside. There were dozens of newspaper clippings about Nate's adventure aboard the *Lusitania*. That was the second time Nate had worked with Houdini on a case: together they exposed and captured a group of terrorists set on shooting former president Teddy Roosevelt. The clippings were from around the world, in languages Nate would never be able to read even if he stayed in school until he was thirty!

Some of the articles were accompanied by photographs taken when the ship had landed in England. In all the pictures, Houdini was smiling. In some, his hand was on Nate's shoulder; in others, Houdini's outstretched hands pointed toward "the real hero, my colleague Nate Fuller."

It was painful to remember that only seconds after those exhilarating moments were captured on film, Houdini learned that his beloved mother had died.

Houdini's devotion to his mother was well known to the public, but outsiders could hardly comprehend the depths of Houdini's feelings. They were forged in child-hood experiences he never shared with anyone. It was Mrs. Houdini who had told Nate the Weiss family history.

Houdini's birth name was Ehrich Weiss. At thirteen— Nate's age—he started supporting his family. Houdini's brothers and sisters were all more or less successful as adults, but Cecilia Weiss lived with the son who had be-come Houdini because he insisted on it. "Mother Weiss" ran the house, and that pleased everyone.

Houdini lavished all the attention and wealth upon his mother that she would tolerate. When the Houdinis took her on a grand European tour, Houdini tracked down every living relative he could find in Austria-Hungary, her birthplace, and brought them to meet her. He offered her expensive jewelry and clothing, but her tastes ran to sim-ple comforts like warm woolen slippers.

Everything just seemed to stop for Houdini when she died. Even now, months later, Houdini's wife didn't want to burden him with the news that the police had come to their home and dragged their employee off to jail. It was clear to Nate that he had to get Ace out of this scrape, whatever it was.

"What in the world did Ace do?" Nate asked Captain Root after they had exchanged hellos in the backseat of his chauffeured police car.

"A very sad affair this is, young Mr. Fuller," the burly old detective said. "When Mrs. Houdini called and said that boy had been arrested, I thought, *This might be the tonic Mr. Houdini needs.* You get my drift? A mother's dying is not to be made light of. But a man like Mr. Houdini— he must be nearly forty!—has to get on with *his* life."

"Standing up for Ace is just what the doctor ordered," Nate agreed, shivering in the unheated police car.

"But . . . things won't play out happily for young Winchell," Root said, then turned and stared sternly at Nate. "Forget that your path ever crossed his: that's my advice to you. I'm going uptown as a friend. I'm telling her not to bother Houdini with this. Just wash your hands clean of Ace Winchell."

"Godfrey Daniel!" Nate said, unconsciously using an expression of Allie's. "You act as though Ace had robbed a bank, or committed a murder."

The detective rubbed his gloved hands briskly and exhaled a long, frosty breath. "He did, in point of fact. He murdered Carl Templeton Cramer. Ace Winchell is the Fifth Avenue Slasher."

"Never," whispered Nate. He sat in stunned silence for . . . he couldn't tell how long, before saying, "You think Ace is the Fifth Avenue Slasher?"

"It's not up to what I think. It's not my case."

"The idea is . . . crazy. Ace couldn't have done anything like *that*."

"It's not my case, but a boy with his past, from his neighborhood—can you say it's not possible?"

"You bet I can," Nate said defiantly. "I just had lunch with him today, only hours ago. I certainly would have known if I was having an egg salad sandwich with someone responsible for the Crime of the Decade."

"Only the *Tribune* is calling it the Crime of the Decade. Other papers make it the Crime of the Century. And it's only 1911. That's reaching, if you ask me," the captain joked.

Houdini called that "typical gallows humor"—the way policemen make jokes about the horrible things they see every day on the job, to prevent themselves from feeling all the pain and suffering of others. But this was *Ace*. In life-or-death trouble. Nate didn't want people joking about it.

Still, why should a policeman be sympathetic? People were screaming for the capture of the Fifth Avenue Slasher. Every day that had passed since the murder brought wilder press accusations about the careless, inept police investigation. Even cover-ups were mentioned. This crime had touched a nerve like no other. The Fifth Avenue murder had caused more public outcry than the recent shooting of Mayor Gaynor.

Why? The mayor is more famous than Mr. Cramer. But Mayor Gaynor survived, with the bullet still in him.

Still, murder was common on the Lower East Side and

in other poor neighborhoods. Murders there never made headlines. Dying poor wasn't newsworthy, Nate guessed.

But Cramer's being rich and famous was only part of the story. The murder's brutality, the victim's fame and generosity to charity, the nearness of Christmas—they all contributed to the public outrage. Maybe the most important factor was that Cramer had been tortured and killed in his own home, his castle.

Yes, he was a king of commerce who had lived inside the walls of his own stone fortress. But it wasn't enough to keep one savage out. And by tomorrow millions of people will think Ace is that savage.

"It takes getting used to, seeing that you call him a friend," the captain said unexpectedly.

Nate nodded weakly. He knew in his heart that he would never believe it.

BRUTAL MURDER ON EAST 54TH STREET

7

Mrs. Houdini had been waiting at the door. She ushered them into the parlor, took her place by the fire, and asked to be told the worst. It hit her like a body blow from a heavyweight champion. Even seated she staggered, speechless.

"Captain, what is the evidence against Ace?" Nate asked. "It has to be circumstantial at best."

"Don't look down your nose at circumstantial evidence. Very few murderers are caught red-handed with a bloody knife, but many get the hot seat up at Sing Sing," the captain replied.

The vision of Ace's hair catching on fire gave Nate a jolt. He knew that even though the modern, improved electric chair was better designed than Houdini's antique, some prisoners still burst into flames from too much current going through their bodies.

"But Ace has to be too young to be executed!" he protested.

"Most hold that if someone is old enough to do murder, he's old enough to fry for it," Captain Root declared.

"Ace did no such thing; he is innocent," Mrs. Houdini said. "I *know* this because my husband would never hire a violent criminal—a gang member—to work for us . . . in our home."

"Wilhelmina, my champion! You are correct as always. I did not hire a gang member. *Or* a killer."

"Houdini!" said three surprised voices as one. Mrs. Houdini had assured her guests that there was no hope of seeing or hearing the world-famed escape artist, but suddenly, here he was, right in their midst.

"Many thanks to you, Captain—for alerting us to this . . . infamous injustice—"

"That's what it is," Nate agreed, "an *infamous injustice*!"

"And thanks for bringing Ace's champion to our home," Houdini said as he crossed the room and affectionately squeezed Nate's shoulders with his powerful hands.

Nate was shocked by Houdini's appearance. That he was not in a fresh shirt and coat was unsurprising. Mrs. Houdini always had to badger him about looking presentable when he was not onstage. No, it was Houdini's careworn face that stunned Nate. The habitual smile was absent. A sad man was staring down, working hard at being sociable.

"I am sorry for your loss. Extremely sorry," Root said in his consoling policeman's voice.

Houdini uncharacteristically mumbled his words of thanks. He glanced at a picture of himself, Bess, and his mother on the mantelpiece and softly sighed.

"My mother and I feel the same way," Nate said sympathetically. "Aunt Alice, too."

"I can't seem to get over it," Houdini said to the picture. "Sometimes I feel all right and a moment later am as bad as ever. Time heals all wounds, but a *long* time will have to pass to heal this wound."

"This is too hard for you," Mrs. Houdini said.

"I fear that I have made it even harder for you, my adorable sunshine . . . I must try to cheer up," he said with determination. "Must try to be a man for Bess. And now for Ace."

Houdini wheeled around to face his guests. "So how is Ace being framed? That's the question."

"Framed?" Root objected. "You're not accusing us, are you? It's a solid case against him."

"Be so kind, Captain, as to lay it before us," Houdini requested.

"It's like this, sir. Mr. Cramer's man—his butler-valet type—gave us a detailed description of everything that went missing the night of the murder. That's including

45

the personal items. So, we knew the color of his billfold, the make of his watch, and the look of his rings *and* his monogrammed cigar case. We gave that list to every pawnbroker and fence in the city."

"Why should a *fence* help, since they are criminals themselves?" Mrs. Houdini asked. "Or am I mistaken?"

"You're right, ma'am, technically—but fences 'assist' criminals more than being criminals themselves. Anyway, the promise of a free pass for fencing this merchandise *and* a thousand-dollar reward buys a lot of cooperation," Captain Root explained.

"I have no doubt," Houdini said. A startling transformation was taking place. Houdini had become taut, alert. His body seemed to grow inside his clothing. A light flickered in his eyes, the effect like coal reigniting a smoldering fire.

"Worked like a charm. Honest Bill Gates called a patrolman into his store on Chrystie Street last night and showed him a red-leather cigar case with the initials C.T.C. on it. He swore that he had no idea it was stolen goods when he gave Ace Winchell seven dollars for it."

"Honest Bill. The name screams insincerity," Houdini observed.

"And it wasn't just Bill. His son, Bill Junior, was there, too, when Ace Winchell sold the victim's cigar case."

"There could be dozens of reasons for Ace to have had that case, Captain," Nate said. "He might have been selling it for a friend—the real murderer. Or he might have found it in the street. Or—"

"Or he might never 'a' seen the cigar case in the first place. And he never walked into Honest Bill's used clothing store last night," the captain added sarcastically.

"Is that what he claims? You've spoken with Ace?" Houdini asked.

"That's exactly what he claims. When I heard that Ace Winchell was the Fifth Avenue Slasher, I thought I owed it to Mr. Houdini to walk over to the Tombs and hear the boy's side of the story."

Nate knew the fearsome reputation of the Halls of Justice, the city's main prison. Jailhouse wits said the Tombs was where the city buried the guilty and the guiltless together.

"Claims he never laid eyes on the cigar case, never went into Gates's store . . . never heard of Cramer, let alone killed the man," Root said.

"I told you that he is innocent," Mrs. Houdini said.

Root exhaled deeply again and gathered his thoughts.

"Everyone we arrest says he is innocent, ma'am. Every blessed one of them. But when a *solid citizen* comes forward with hard evidence and a believable story, we have to do something."

"Why is Gates's word better than Ace's?" Nate asked.

"For starters, because Honest Bill Gates is the *Mayor* of Chrystie Street!"

Nate scrunched his eyes in confusion.

"You wouldn't know much about street mayors, living in a town house at Fifty-third off of Madison. On the Lower East Side, it seems like there are more mayors than streets," the captain explained with a laugh.

"What do these street mayors do?" Nate asked.

"They're fixers, and they grease the wheels. They get out the vote for Tammany Hall, they find jobs and apartments for people. And they keep track of troublemakers for the local precinct—tell us if a boy we arrest deserves a second chance, or if he belongs in the pen like Winchell does."

"Certainly Ace, living in the neighborhood, knows that Gates has a semiofficial position," Houdini pointed out. "Why go to him with such incriminating evidence?"

"Because he's the best fence on the Bowery. Pays more for stolen goods than anybody else in the district," Captain Root replied. "That's why they call him Honest Bill Gates."

"So a criminal's word is taken for truth before the word of a hardworking boy who supports his family," Mrs. Houdini complained, practically taking the words out of Nate's mouth.

"Please, return to my original concern—why dispose of an item every policeman in the city is on the lookout for?" Houdini asked.

"Why do any of them do stupid things, sir? Desperate for a drink. For a fancy suit. Or a present for a girlfriend."

"Captain, that's all wet," Nate said. "Ace doesn't have a girlfriend. He doesn't need new clothes. Why, he insisted on buying lunch for me and Al— for me *and* someone else this afternoon."

"Proceeds of fencing the cigar case, is my guess."

"Captain, I tell you that Ace earns enough working for my husband that he did not need seven dollars to feed some secret vice he does not have," Mrs. Houdini said firmly.

"Ma'am, it don't really matter *why* he did it. The fact is he did it. And the D.A. thinks that'll be plenty for a jury."

A distant telephone rang. Houdini jumped up and theatrically gestured stop with both arms. "Hold that thought. Bess, please offer our guests refreshments while I take the phone in my library."

8

Before long, Hilde the cook appeared, laying out a feast for the Houdinis' guests: coffee, tea, milk, cream, and a magnificent-looking chocolate cake so heavy she wheeled it in on a trolley.

"Don't wait for my husband, he has no appetite these days," said their hostess.

Nate's first forkful of Hilde's cake nearly made him forget the case. Chocolate pudding inside the cake was infused with shredded coconut and slivered nuts. No cook in his house had ever made a dessert like this; Aunt Alice favored stewed prunes.

Houdini returned in midsentence: ". . . a single piece of physical evidence and the testimony of questionable witnesses. Very thin. Is that"—the entertainer paused and demonstrated a paper-thin space between his thumb and opposing index finger—"is *that* sufficient to send a boy to his death?"

"But *all* the evidence is against your friend," the captain told him.

"That *all* is practically nothing, in my humble opinion."

"Tell us why you think Ace is innocent," Nate said.

"Considering the matter for only these few moments, already I could write a book. But, to the point. First, Ace pursued *some* criminal activity, before he became an honest, productive citizen. That was years ago, when he was a mere *child*. Second, breaking and entering is a skill that takes time to acquire. He was not a second-story man *then*; how did he become one overnight?

"Third, if Ace needed the paltry sum of seven dollars, he could have thrown damning evidence like that cigar case in the East River and come to me for an advance on salary or asked for a loan from a co-worker or—"

"From me," Nate added.

"Precisely. Now then, fourth. With due modesty, I am an unexcelled judge of character. I think Ace is capable, with provocation, of doing bodily harm. But he is not capable of torturing a helpless man, nor of slitting his throat, nor of robbing his corpse."

"That's enough for me," Nate said. "What about you, Captain?"

"Mr. Houdini is preaching to the wrong congregation, if you get my drift. The police work is done. You have to convince the district attorney that Ace is innocent."

"And he has his eyes on a higher office," Houdini noted.

"Was there ever a politician that didn't?" Root joked.

"Even if convicting Ace would help the D.A.'s career, he has to listen to us," Nate said. "He wouldn't risk convicting the wrong man."

"It's certainly good to see you haven't lost your sense of humor, Mr. Fuller," the captain said. "A quick conviction—and execution—is worth a million votes."

"So, this small but worthy band must champion Ace's cause," Houdini said grandly.

"Count me out, sir," Captain Root replied. "I came here to fill you in—strictly out of friendship. This never was my case, and now it's the D.A.'s."

"Well then, it is good that Ace has the best legal team working for him," Houdini said.

"How did Ace get a lawyer?" Nate asked eagerly.

"I hired him. Miles, of Miles, Dewey and Davis."

"First-rate choice," Captain Root said. "Pricey though."

"Was that Mr. Miles who just called?" Mrs. Houdini asked.

"It was."

"How did he get your number, Houdini? Mental telepathy?"

"No, I called him . . . after I overheard you telling

Hilde about Ace's arrest," Houdini said a bit sheepishly as his wife eyed him closely.

"From what I gathered, Ace had already been taken away. I proceeded the most practical way possible—hiring an attorney and having him meet with Ace before he was even fingerprinted."

"Phew! I'll bet they loved that downtown," said the captain.

"Quite. Mr. Miles told me that District Attorney Whitman had a pack of headline-starved reporters and photographers ready to watch him march the Fifth Avenue Slasher into booking. But Miles arrived before Ace and the detectives—they had a flat tire on the way, poor devils—and it was more like a hurricane than merely rain on the D.A.'s parade."

"Can we visit Ace today?" Nate asked eagerly.

"Visiting hours end at four," the captain said, "but you won't be able to see him until after he's charged."

"Which will not be until all the press is reassembled there tomorrow morning," Houdini said.

"Shouldn't we be there, to give him moral support?" Nate asked.

"No, regrettably," Houdini said very firmly. "Once the press ties Houdini to Ace, they will hound me. I won't be able to breathe without flash powder exploding. Under those circumstances, how could I possibly hope to prove Ace's innocence? Therefore, we stay away for the moment."

Nate knew Houdini was right. Anything Houdini did in public sold newspapers. Linking the most famous man in America to the most infamous criminal—poor Ace!— would be like striking gold, silver, and diamonds in the same shovelful of dirt.

"I shall contact people I know," Houdini said with an air of mystery. "I will call in favors, ferret out as much as possible. Then we will gather again—regrettably, without you, Captain—and see how to proceed. Agreed?"

Nate agreed. What choice did he have? He had no better alternative plan, which left him feeling completely frustrated. At least Houdini suggested sending messages, via the lawyer, to bolster Ace's spirits. Mrs. Houdini, with a shaking hand, wrote a letter that she didn't share with anyone. Nate wrote a quick note himself:

Dear Ace,

We all know that you didn't do it—any of it. Keep your chin up. We will be doing everything we can to clear you.

See you on visiting day. Until then, I am

Your friend,

Nate Fuller

P.S. Houdini has resurfaced and is taking charge. He hired your lawyer, Mr. Miles. Do everything Mr. Miles recommends. Captain Root called him "first-rate." And "pricey."

After bidding their hosts good night, Nate and the captain were driven downtown. They rode in silence until the captain said, "Houdini has convinced himself that Ace is being framed. I don't see it."

"But *you* disliked Ace from the moment that you met him," Nate argued, recalling a run-in Ace and Captain Root had had the previous summer.

"That's as may be. I can't change the past, can I?" the detective said apologetically. "But that doesn't make him innocent in this matter. I have a pretty good nose for villains, you know."

"I wish that you would use your nose on that Honest Bill Gates. Make him tell the truth. Give him the third degree."

"Mr. Fuller, *my* boss says the case is closed. I won't go kicking up dust because you say your friend was framed. I won't."

Root won't. Houdini can't. I guess that just leaves me.

9

Nate looked up from his cornflakes and stared in amazement at the little girl—his cousin—happily eating breakfast across the table from him. Her sudden appearance had caused Nate's mother to ignore her flu and take Allie under her wing like a daughter. That was unexpected, but not amazing.

It *was* amazing that Allie seemed to have cured Aunt Alice as well. The discovery of a previously unknown niece had turned Aunt Alice into a dynamo.

According to Marina, Aunt Alice had stormed into her room before dawn saying, "I am well, so you are well, too. Breakfast will be ready at eight." Then Aunt Alice went to Bea's room and told her to have a hansom cab waiting outside at ten. Finally, she called on Allie and told her that buying a wardrobe suitable to New York in December was their goal for the day.

Nate couldn't have planned things any better than Aunt Alice already had. Since he was not invited on the ladies' shopping adventure, he was left free for important detective work. And Nate's mother was so thrilled about the upcoming excursion that she didn't need to know he would be ducking out for a few hours on Ace's behalf.

A good thing, too, since Nate had pored over the bad news before coming to breakfast. The newspaper's front page featured a two-column picture of Ace and banner headlines:

FIFTH AVENUE SLASHER ARRESTED
CITYWIDE MANHUNT SUCCEEDS
DISTRICT ATTORNEY PREDICTS
SPEEDY CONVICTION

One story had an interview with William Gates, a self-proclaimed "gentleman's tailor of Chrystie Street." *That's rich,* Nate thought.

Gates had told the newspaper how he helped crack the case: "I've known the boy all his life, and always known he was bad. When he came in with something of value to sell, I knew it had to be stolen."

You rat! Your stock-in-trade is stolen merchandise.

"If more people did their civic duty and turned in

hooligans like Winchell, our city would be a safer, happier place."

That's the limit, Nate thought after he hid the newspaper in his sock drawer and went down to breakfast. *We'll really be safer and happier when you tell the truth.*

"I do believe you haven't heard a single word I've been saying," Allie said from across the table.

"I guess I haven't. What have you been saying?"

"I've been saying that you should come with us. I bet that Aunt Alice would buy you a new outfit, too."

"Oh, I know you're wrong there. You are going to stores that sell ladies' clothes. I go to stores for men."

She looked at him skeptically and asked, "Is that really true? Some stores for ladies and other stores just for men?"

"You bet. This is a big, wonderful, exciting city. Let Aunt Alice treat you to it today."

"But I'm going feel bad that you're here all by yourself, Cousin," she said with lavish concern.

"I won't be bored, believe me," he said, itching to start his investigation.

10

Nate walked toward the exit of the elevated train station and scanned the street below him. It seemed at first that every storefront on the Bowery housed either a bar or a men's clothing store. At street level, he realized that they had the largest signs. Sandwiched in between were tattoo parlors, pawnshops, fortune-tellers, a dime museum, and a number of places offering "beds by the night." One advertised its prices: COTS—10 CENTS, HAMMOCKS—7 CENTS, FLOOR—A NICKEL.

The Bowery was unlike any other New York avenue—and everyone knew it. It drew tourists from all over the country who were looking for something sinful to do. No wonder it was also home to an army of petty thieves, pickpockets, and con artists. Watching the bustling human traffic, Nate thought of the old saying that you could stand exactly where he stood and fire a shotgun in any direction with no fear of injuring an honest man.

He walked urgently to Chrystie Street and turned toward his destination, a banner proclaiming HONEST BILL GATES, TAILOR, ONLY THE BEST NEW & SECOND HAND CLOTHING.

A "spieler" worked the street outside the store. He had just grabbed hold of a passerby and was trying to get him inside with a nonstop sales pitch: "On special today, my friend. A two-piece, no vest, built like a rock. No charge for looking—cheap, cheap, cheap. Quick come, quick go. Get it now."

The spieler sized Nate up and immediately involved him in the patter.

"Mister, now look at this handsome young man. And those high-quality threads he's wearing. Don't you know that he shops here at Honest Bill's? Nowhere else can you get this kind of quality."

Nate slid behind him and through the door. Four rows of clothes racks ran the length of the narrow, rectangular room. He noticed shirts, pants, suits, and coats all mixed together on the racks, which were distinguished from one another only by handwritten signs saying LARGE, REGULAR, and BOYS. The walls on either side of the room had shelves crammed with other merchandise. There were porcelain statues, pots and pans, picture frames, musical instruments, display cases with jewelry. Just an overwhelming array, and none of it looked valuable.

"You buyin' or just borrowin' steam heat?" a hostile voice said over his shoulder—it was a guard protecting the merchandise. Nate smiled and walked between two racks. Looking around, he saw a man standing on a balcony at the rear wall. None other than Honest Bill Gates himself, Nate decided.

Gates was dressed to the teeth in a light brown windowpane-checked suit over a beige checked vest. A shiny brown derby topped a dome of fiery red hair and a thickly freckled face. With hands in pockets, hips thrust forward, and a cigar stub clamped in his jaw, Honest Bill seemed ready to go a few rounds with any customer.

We'll see if he's up to sparring with Houdini and me, Nate thought as the proprietor moseyed down the balcony steps and strutted toward him.

"You're in the right place now. You'll walk out of Honest Bill's with everything you desire, young man," Gates promised. "And your pocketbook won't be empty, neither."

"That's quite a promise. I hope you're one hundred percent correct," Nate said, unintentionally repeating one of Houdini's favorite phrases.

"I think you're here shopping for your father's Christmas present. Maybe a brother? What are we looking for?"

"I'm shopping for my cousin, my girl cousin actually," Nate replied.

"Girl?"

"Because I had heard you have jewelry—fancy jewelry—at good prices."

As Gates looked suspiciously at his well-tailored duds, Nate added, "A kid who works with me at Macy's said I could get something cheap here that looks nice. Don't be fooled by my clothes, I'm just a store clerk myself."

"I can't say that I didn't wonder what you were doing here, wearing a suit like that," Gates said, pointing with his cigar butt for emphasis. "I ain't Tiffany's, you know."

"My husband has too big a heart," said a modestly dressed woman who popped out from behind a clothing rack. "Neighborhood people bring things when they need money to pay a bill or buy medicine. A pawnbroker only gives them what it's worth—which is nothing for most of it."

"We'd throw it out," Gates said, holding a brass flute bent into a soft U-shape, "but people would just drag it right out of the garbage and sell it to us again."

"You must make up for your losses on the stolen property you buy and sell," Nate blurted angrily, tipping his hand.

"Who are you that you accuse my husband of being a criminal?"

"Oh, nobody really. I'd just heard that you deal in better merchandise than what's here."

"Your friend told you, eh? What's his name, this friend from Macy's?" Gates asked sharply.

Regretting that he couldn't back up, Nate plunged ahead.

"Ace Winchell is my friend's name, the guy you're framing for murder."

Husband and wife both looked a bit stunned, but neither broke down and confessed. They turned toward each other and whispered words Nate couldn't hear. He did observe a young clerk edging up behind them, straining to eavesdrop. The clerk had Gates's fiery red hair and deeply freckled skin—*Bill Junior,* Nate decided. *The other witness.*

"It must be a terrible, terrible thing to find out someone you care about, like your friend, isn't the person you thought he was," Mrs. Gates said with feeling.

"That's enough, Edith. The kid is leaving," said Honest Bill, planting his cigar stub in the corner of his mouth. Mrs. Gates turned obediently away and was visibly surprised to see her son. She grabbed Bill Junior by the arm and forced him to leave with her. Nate could see all this without taking his eyes off the store owner.

"Why are you really here? Who the hell sent you?" Gates demanded.

"I'm here to get the truth."

"Who says I'm not telling the truth? They're damn liars, whoever they are!"

"I'm not going to reveal my sources. Why should I?" Nate said, playing for time. "But you should think about the fact that I'm not the only one who knows what really happened."

"Is that so?"

"It is," Nate said, fervently hoping his own lies were convincing. "And it will go easier on you—in the long run—if you tell the truth and admit your story about Ace is bunk."

Gates took the cigar stub from his mouth very deliberately. He looked down and spat tobacco juice on Nate's right shoe and pant leg.

"That's all you're getting from me today, kid. If you think I'm lying, go tell the D.A."

"You bet I will."

"Oscar, show this lousy snoop the sidewalk," Gates told the security guard as he turned and walked away.

11

Nate was still rubbing the hip he had landed on when he arrived at the Houdinis' brownstone. Before ringing the doorbell, he shot a quick glance behind, hoping at last to glimpse the person who had tailed him from the Bowery all the way to the Upper West Side. He might have seen the same head of red hair more than once, out of the corner of his eye. Or maybe he just had red hair on the brain after confronting the Gateses.

Houdini greeted Nate at the door and ushered him into his study. Noticing the boy's limp, Houdini postponed any discussion until he had given Nate an ice pack to sit on.

While Nate related his morning's activities in minute

detail, Houdini leaned back in his office chair and removed his shoes and socks. He then opened a fresh deck of playing cards and proceeded to cut and shuffle them between his sockless toes. All the while Houdini never took his eyes off Nate. When they first met, Nate had been disconcerted by talking while the entertainer manipulated magic props. Now he barely noticed.

"I cannot fault the man for ejecting you," Houdini noted. "You did walk into his store and spit in his eye, so to speak—calling him a liar."

Nate looked at his stained pant leg but resisted saying the obvious about who did the spitting. "Don't you think his actions *absolutely proved* that he's lying?"

"One hundred percent!" Houdini agreed. "He should have pitied you as a feebleminded do-gooder—if his indictment of Ace was truthful. That he became so agitated tells me the story is a total falsehood. No doubt now—Ace is being deliberately framed."

"What is Gates's motive?"

"Aah, we don't know enough even to guess."

"Maybe Ace has some idea?" Nate suggested hopefully, wanting to see his unfortunate friend.

"We will ask when we visit, of course."

"Today?"

"Not today," Houdini said after glancing at the wall clock in his office. "Mr. Miles said that a few reporters are suspicious about who is footing Ace's legal bill. It's only a matter of time before my involvement in the case becomes public, but we don't need to hasten this discovery."

Houdini neatly put all the cards back in a box on his desk using only his toes and said, "Let's strike while we still have surprise on our side, my friend. Interviewing a notorious criminal acquaintance of mine may help us advance Ace's cause."

The mystical entertainer made a short phone call while putting on his shoes, said goodbye to Mrs. Houdini in her sewing room, leashed Charlie the terrier, and bounced toward the front door. Charlie yapped and leaped for joy at the prospect of an outing with his master.

Outside, an expensive touring car—the type that waited in front of Fifth Avenue mansions—idled in the street. Seeing Houdini and Charlie bounding toward it, the driver opened his door. Houdini rushed to block the door with his body before the driver could get out. Charlie barked, but not threateningly; Houdini's dog obviously recognized the driver.

"Frankie, pretending to be a chauffeur will *not* do."

"You are an *im-por-tant* man," the gray-haired chap said in a thick Italian accent. "You need someone to open doors for you."

"Frankie, I have been opening doors for myself since I was a baby . . . and have made a pretty fine job of it so far," Houdini joked, taking a seat in the passenger compartment, Charlie nuzzling in alongside his master. "Nate

Fuller, this is my friend and neighbor Frankie Bonamino. He insists on driving me to the cemetery—in Queens—whenever I wish to visit my mother's resting place."

"It's my pleasure. I love to drive, and Houdini is good company," Frankie replied in a musical voice that rose and fell and rose again. "You work for Houdini?"

"No, sir, I'm . . . in school," Nate said, feeling a little foolish as he clambered into the backseat next to Houdini. He was about to add that he was in the crime-solving business, but thought better of it.

"Nate is a resourceful associate in dangerous situations," Houdini said.

"I am pleased to meet you then, Nate."

"The pleasure is mutual, Mr. Bonamino."

"Frankie is also a friend of Ace's," Houdini said.

"That's right. Ace is a good boy. Houdini keeps him very, very busy, but he finds time to run errands and write letters for us. Our English is not too fine, but Ace's is *perfecto*. And what manners. Not like those *brutes* who took the boy to jail. They said they would arrest me, too, if I did not shut up."

Hearing about the excellence of Ace's character reignited Nate's fury over his arrest.

"How can the police be so *dim*? To think Ace could—"

"In the old country, only a fool believes the police," Frankie said. "Steal a little, go to jail; steal a lot, make a career of it."

"Ace's problems do not originate with the police," Houdini said firmly.

"I guess Bill Gates's statement was all the reason they needed to charge Ace," Nate said.

"And so, disproving that statement is paramount. Frankie, be so kind as to point this machine toward Bowery and Stanton. Nate and I will walk from there."

Houdini rubbed his hands vigorously and said, "Now to business; my sources have given me valuable background about dear Mr. Gates."

Nate didn't ask who these sources were; Houdini would have told him if he could.

"Gates was made Mayor of Chrystie Street by the most powerful criminal kingpin the city has ever seen, Mad Max Eastman. Gates was skillful enough to survive Eastman's fall."

"Eastman died?" Nate asked.

"No, he took a stupid pill and got sent to the joint, as they say in his neighborhood. Before that, Mad Max ran the Bowery district with an iron fist for fifteen years. Eastman's gang was the largest criminal organization in the country. It operated a dozen different rackets."

"Was Ace a member of Eastman's gang?" Nate asked.

"A logical question, Nate. Eastman controlled—and profited from—the crimes of at least two thousand men, women, and children. But he interacted with only three—his top lieutenants. The youthful Ace was a member of a subgang called the Squab Wheelmen. Crazy Butch McGurk, one of Eastman's big three, was the gang's leader."

"How could Ace get involved with men like that?"

"Gangs are the basic social unit in tenement neighborhoods, Nate. It would have been almost *unnatural* if Ace had not become a gang member when he was eleven or twelve—for survival."

"It's hard to imagine," Nate said. "There are no gangs where I live. Certainly none in my school."

"East Fifty-third Street is a world away from the Bowery."

"I guess it is," Nate said. "Does this Crazy Butch run all the gangs now that Eastman's upriver?"

"No. No one does. Eastman had three lieutenants: Crazy Butch, Kid Twist, and Louie the Lump. All of them made plays for control, but nobody ever got the upper hand for long. So today they share the Bowery, from Fourth Avenue in the north to Chinatown in the south. They share, and they circle each other like dogs competing for the same bone."

"We're going to see one of them?"

"Pardon me, but no! We're going to see their old boss. I learned this morning that Mad Max Eastman is out of prison and operating his old business," Houdini said.

"He's already running the gangs again?" Nate asked loudly enough to wake the dozing terrier.

"You'll see soon enough—both of you," Houdini said,

scratching his pet's chin and smiling impishly as he turned to look at Nate. "Eastman did more than lie, steal, and break heads. He trained others to do it for him."

"Just what *is* a Squab Wheelman, Houdini?"

"He was a key part of Eastman's bicycle business. Mad Max *required* that his employees rent bicycles from him every week. Unbelievably, some employees used those bicycles to steal."

"How can somebody use a bicycle to steal?" Nate asked.

Houdini explained that on a crowded street, a young boy—possibly our friend Ace—would apparently lose control of his bicycle and run into an elderly woman. The boy would cry out for help, and a crowd would rush to the injured woman's assistance. While the Good Samaritans milled about, their pockets and purses were picked by a gang of children mingling in the melee. After Ace apologized and pedaled away, he would meet his accomplices— who had also fled on Mad Max's bicycles—and divide the spoils far from the scene of their crime.

"It was a smooth trick, all right," Houdini commented. "Max made money both ways. He got a percentage of the take and the rental fee."

Nate shook his head.

Just then, Frankie swerved, nearly swiping another car at an intersection. Making notes in the car proved a challenge; this was the first of many such encounters as their car made its way downtown.

12

Nate and Houdini left Frankie Bonamino at the corner of Bowery and Stanton with his motor running—he refused to return home without them—and headed toward Chrystie Street.

Charlie was eager for excitement. The dog tugged at his leash, sniffing and digging—curiously exploring new territory. Nate was familiar with side streets like Chrystie from running errands in the neighborhood, part of his job the previous summer. It was where the people who worked and shopped on the Bowery lived—a tenement block. Frozen laundry hung on clotheslines stretched all the way from dilapidated buildings on one side of the street to equally decrepit structures on the other side. The odor of rotting garbage was only partially masked by the snow and frigid air. Near a corner bar, a group of boys younger than Nate huddled against the cold, smoking cigarettes and making catcalls about the millionaires and their limousine. None had overcoats or winter boots.

Houdini approached a door decorated with a scraggily wreath, the only Christmas decoration Nate noticed on the block. A faded painted sign above announced:

MAX EASTMAN'S ANIMAL EMPORIUM
CATS FOR SALE & BIRDS OF ALL KINDS
ESTABLISHED 1897

An unoiled hinge screeched when Houdini opened the door and stepped inside. Charlie barked as he trotted in, triggering a cascade of animal anger and panic. The walls of Eastman's store were lined with cages—cats on the left and birds on the right. The caged cats arched their backs. They hissed and snarled, but they were calm compared with the hundreds of fearful birds, who flapped and fluttered and made an overwhelming din of squawking noises. Charlie, enjoying the reception, lolled his tongue and barked in return.

A mountainous man burst through a rear door and boomed out, "What are you, stupid? Get that dog outta here double-quick or I'll give you lumps to die from."

The man spoke soothing phrases and moved from cage to cage—begging the agitated birds and cats to calm down.

Mad Max Eastman towered over Nate and Houdini, and he certainly weighed more than both of them together. But all that weight was muscle, which Nate could see since he wore only an undershirt and Levi's.

As the chaos diminished, Eastman's face suddenly lit up.

"Houdini, is that you? Hully Gee, it is! You know better than to bring your mutt in here."

"It never occurred to me, Mad Max," Houdini said innocently.

"Right! Just like Mayor Gaynor and I had tea yesterday," Eastman said. "And you know that 'Mad' is just to impress rubes," he said, pointing them toward his office through the door in the back.

They followed, although Charlie was reluctant. He had to be pulled away from his new friends. Inside his office, Eastman waved Houdini and Nate to rickety wooden chairs around a circular table.

"Max, I take it you're not a fan of our reform-minded mayor," Houdini said.

"After he fired a dozen boys *my* mayors put into City Hall jobs, some of them relatives! He should eat nothing but the dirt in the street."

"Isn't placing qualified candidates in city jobs good for everyone, sir?" Nate asked uncertainly.

"How can some churchified Brooklyn judge know what's good for real people? Go on! You think he cares about who needs a job on Chrystie Street? Who needs help with the rent on Broome? What building on Essex needs a coal delivery on the cuff?"

"But the mayor was elected to represent all the people, not just those on the Lower East Side."

"Gawd. You sound like a banker. You J. P. Morgan's boy?"

"Hardly, Max. Nate is my associate," Houdini said.

Eastman inspected Nate thoroughly before commenting, "He's a good-lookin' boy. A bit scrawny though."

"Pleased to meet you, too," Nate muttered, but the gangster paid no attention. He grabbed a whiskey bottle from a shelf at the side of the room and waved it toward Houdini.

"Hair of the dog?" he asked. When Houdini declined, Eastman said, "Bless the saints, it's never too early for me."

He poured a generous glass of brown liquor, slammed the bottle on the table, and planted himself firmly in the chair nearest Nate. The man who once commanded the most feared criminal organization in the country then sipped his whiskey daintily, as if it were tea.

Stop staring, Nate told himself. But he found it impossible not to stare. Up close, Nate saw that all shapes of scars—from circles to long slashes—marked Eastman's arms and face. The gangster's nose had been so badly broken that it pointed sideways. Purple veins stood out on his face and forehead. Long, uncombed black hair draped over his thick neck. Amazingly, Eastman's head was bullet-shaped—a description Nate had read but never personally seen. And the crowning touch *was* the man's crown: a dusty, battered brown derby that perched uncertainly on the side of his head.

Eastman rose and restlessly walked around the table. Without warning, he grabbed Houdini's shoulder and squeezed ferociously. Houdini acted as if he didn't notice.

"Your stay upriver didn't do you any harm I see," Houdini said as he pried the giant's hand from his shoulder.

"Aah, I'm a washed-up old bum. You know I'm out of the game, right? I just run the pet store."

"I've heard that rumor," Houdini said.

"It's gospel. Keepin' my nose clean. Let them young bucks have the grief, that's what I say."

"And they pay you nicely to stay out of their business?"

"If they do, that's between me and my pocketbook," Eastman said. "Don't go starting no rumors that get me in Dutch with the law."

"That's the furthest thing from my mind," Houdini promised.

Eastman sat and poured another glassful from his whiskey bottle. "Is this a social call? Or you here to buy a bird? I know you got some at home."

The Houdinis did have a floor-to-ceiling aviary in their

kitchen, but Nate wondered how Mad Max would know that.

Has Eastman ever been to Houdini's home?

"Max, I need to plumb your encyclopedic knowledge of this neighborhood," Houdini said.

"I'm all ears."

Only a tiny exaggeration, Nate observed. Eastman's ears were large and discolored—probably from too many bare-knuckled fights.

Houdini popped up, turned his chair around, and settled back down with his arms on the chair back.

"Have another drink, Max. We could be here awhile."

13

"You've heard of Leslie Winchell? Called Ace on the streets?" Houdini asked. "A former member of Butch McGurk's gang, the Squab Wheelmen?"

"A jack-of-all-evil, if I remember," Eastman reflected, "a mug that could break a leg or run a con or pick any pocket."

"Butch thought that Ace could do all that?" Houdini asked.

"Crazy Butch said the kid had potential—maybe enough to even pay off the family debt."

"Family debt?" Houdini asked. "I'm fascinated."

"Well, talk to McGurk about it then," Max said, obviously regretting his slip.

"But what—"

"Butch's private business ain't got nothing to do with me. Talk with him about that. As far as the kid's future, McGurk had plans for him—running a crew, then a saloon. Maybe even the city council."

"But Ace had other plans, didn't he?" Nate said, more as a challenge than a question.

"That's right," Eastman said, taking a gulp, rather than a sip, of liquor. "And how did that work out? Seems I just read about him in the papers. He's going to get all lit up some Saturday night. Get his hair set on fire, maybe."

"Back to Ace and Crazy Butch for a moment?" Houdini asked. "If Ace had such a promising career ahead of him in crime, it must have surprised—shocked—Butch when he quit the gang to go legit."

"Disappointed Butch terrible it did. I mean, after you give a boy every opportunity to make something of his life—"

"Something like the opportunity to become a hunted criminal and spend his life on the run or in jail," Nate blurted out.

"What the . . . ?" Eastman's face contorted. He looked at Nate like he was lower than the droppings on the bottom of a birdcage. "There's a thousand kids on the Bowery that would slit your throat, thank you, for the chance to work with Butch. I don't give a rap whose *associate* you are. Mind your manners or I'll thump you something awful."

"Did Butch think Ace might rat him out?" Houdini asked quickly to defuse the gangster's anger.

"Not likely. You gotta know something to rat a guy out, which a kid of his age didn't."

"Of course. He was merely a Squab Wheelman, a villain in training," Houdini said.

Poker-faced, Eastman nodded.

"But the Wheelmen were your operation, weren't they? So you must have known Ace yourself," Houdini said.

Eastman's scars turned an angrier purple than usual. "I knew the mug. But I knew a *thousand* mugs. He was a pet."

"Pet?" Houdini asked.

Eastman nodded at Charlie, lying patiently on the floor next to his owner's chair. "Like a dog. You know? You teach a dog to fetch, to attack. Sure, you pat it on the head and give it treats, but you keep it on a leash."

"And then you let them off their leashes and made them steal," Nate said.

"*Trained* them to steal," Eastman corrected proudly. "The streets would have made them thieves sooner or later. People need to eat. We taught them how to thieve and not get caught. Stealing's a trade, like any other."

"Thieving was just one of the services offered by the Wheelmen," Houdini said to Nate. "As I recall, you charged ten dollars to have your pets shoot someone in the leg, twenty for an arm shot, twenty-five to deliver a bomb or poison a horse—"

"Why would anyone pay to poison a *horse*?"

"Ain't too bright, is he?" Eastman asked Houdini.

"He's not from your neighborhood," Houdini explained.

"Look, kid, say you're running a business on Delancey Street—you deliver coal or vegetables. Then, some tinhorn muscles in on your business, uses his horse and wagon to deliver to your customers, only cheaper. You want to get rid of the competition, so we'd put him out of business. You can't deliver nothing with a dead horse."

"The law of the jungle reigns," Houdini commented.

"The Bowery was no jungle when *I* ran it," Eastman insisted proudly. "My boys had discipline. They knew it was a job. They hit the bricks every day—made collections, filled the contracts, kept records. And gave receipts. *Today* it's a jungle because there's no leadership."

"Why haven't you taken over, now that you're out?" Nate asked. "Wouldn't the neighborhood be improved if Crazy Butch and Louie the Lump and Kid Twist worked for you again?"

"It would. Everybody's tough luck."

"But if those gentlemen combined forces against you, it wouldn't be pretty," Houdini suggested.

"Why jump me? I'm out of the game, and better for it, too."

"It's not better for young Ace. If you still ran the neighborhood, I doubt that he would be locked up today," Houdini said.

When Eastman didn't rise to the bait, Nate jumped in and asked: "How would Mr. Eastman have kept Ace out of jail?"

"I'd wager that if Honest Bill Gates showed that cigar case to a cop *before* telling Mad Max about it—in the old days—Mrs. Gates would already be a widow."

"You think I used to kill people?" Eastman asked innocently.

"I know that you did," Houdini replied stonily. "And you would punish someone like Gates for ratting out one of your own if you were in charge."

"You maybe got a point."

"Thank you," Houdini said pleasantly. "Wouldn't the same hold for Crazy Butch? Butch owns Gates's street now. Therefore, he *owns* Gates. So either Butch told Gates to hand over that cigar case . . . or you did."

"You're too smart for my taste," Eastman said before draining another glass of whiskey.

"Let me try to get something straight," Nate said. "*Did* Gates show you the cigar case? Or did *you* give it to him? I'm not saying that you're really the Slasher, of course, but you might know who—"

"Get outta here!" Eastman screamed. He pushed the table at Houdini, making his nearly empty bottle fly. Alarmed by glass breaking, Charlie woke and barked furiously at the hulking man apparently threatening his master.

"Get out before I hurt the both of you," Eastman

raged, flinging open the office door. "Don't come around trying to do me dirt. I never was a double-crosser, a fink, or a stool pigeon. And I ain't one now."

Houdini scooped Charlie into his arms and joined Nate in leaving Eastman's Animal Emporium at double time.

14

It seems *too* coincidental that a gangster gets out of jail and practically the next day a . . . a business associate of his accuses Ace of murder," Nate said during the ride back to his house.

"*Far* too coincidental," Houdini agreed.

"We know that Gates's story is a lie. Did Eastman put him up to it?"

"That's a question better answered by crystal ball gazing. Or a Ouija board."

"You don't buy that kind of stuff," Nate protested.

"But I have no better answer to your question than they would offer—at this point. Facts, Nate? Facts?"

"We don't have enough," Nate answered.

"Not nearly enough to formulate a working hypothesis."

"Then what's next?"

"Christmas!"

"I think he means what are we going to do about Ace?" Frankie Bonamino suggested from behind the wheel.

"My mistake," Houdini said, winking at Nate. "But I cannot change the calendar. Tomorrow is Christmas Eve. If we waltzed in with the killer, his signed confession, his knife, all the loot, *and* a choir of witnesses, we still couldn't get Ace sprung before December twenty-sixth."

"Is tomorrow *really* Christmas Eve?" Nate gulped. The holiday had been foremost in his mind at one time.

"The night of my favorite meal—the seven-fish dinner," Frankie said.

"I didn't know that you celebrated Christmas, Houdini. Being Jewish," Nate said.

"Bah! Christmas is an *American* holiday, like the Fourth of July. Bess and I relish both."

They rode in companionable silence the rest of the way uptown, each staring at the holiday street scenes outside, Frankie humming holiday tunes as he drove. "We're here," Houdini said when the car slid to a stop on Nate's block.

As Nate walked toward his front door, he panicked.

I have no idea what to get a ten-year-old girl for Christmas. None!

Inside, it was quiet and dark but warm. Either Bea or

Marina had recovered enough to shovel coal into the furnace. His mother's blue coat was on the rack, but not Allie's ratty canvas coat. Instead, there was a child's winter coat in bright red with a matching wide-brimmed hat on the hook nearest the door. A footstool was tucked in below so Allie could grab her new clothes by herself.

Singing led Nate toward the kitchen. The lyrics told him it was Allie before he pushed the swinging door:

> Just before the battle the General hears a row;
> He says, "The Yanks are coming, I hear their rifles now."
> He turns around in wonder, and what do you think he sees?
> The Georgia Militia, eating goober peas!
> Peas! Peas! Peas! Peas! Eating goober peas!
> Goodness how delicious, eating goober peas!

Stepping through, Nate was surprised. Allie looked neater, but unbelievably puny, in a brown woolen dress with the collar and sleeves edged in white. She was leaning over an ironing board, pushing the wrinkles out of a tablecloth Nate had spilled soup on the day before and put in the laundry.

Seeing him, Allie gleefully cried out, "C'mon, sing with me," and went back to her work. Peeking behind the ironing board, Nate saw that she was perched on three books of the brand-new Encyclopædia Britannica.

Allie sang the last verse and beamed. "Let's sing it again, together. You know the words."

"Actually, I don't know them. I've never heard the song before."

"Never heard it? For a boy with pencils in his pocket and a roomful of books yonder, there's a lot you don't know," Allie teased.

"Allie, how did you get up high enough to screw the electric iron's plug into the ceiling light socket?"

"Electric iron? That's what you call it? I never seen the like of it in Georgia. When I found this iron with a cord coming out of it, it confused me for a while. But then I said the end of the cord is twisty metal just like the end of a lightbulb. So I piled up some of your books on this table, climbed on, twisted out one of the lightbulbs, and twisted in the iron. And sure enough, that iron got red hot. Hotter than it would sitting on a woodstove."

"You could have broken your neck doing that," Nate scolded. "You're too . . . short to be using electric appliances."

"Who says?" she asked defiantly.

"It's obvious. If you can't reach the plug, you are too short to use them."

"Do you have some I'm not too little for?"

"We have more—"

"Mother of Pearl! Show me!" Allie said, clasping her hands together.

"But you're too *young* to use them."

87

Disappointed, she said, "But you can tell me what they are, even if I can't touch them, right?"

"We have an electric toaster and an electric clothes washer, and Marina, the cook, has electric fans. She keeps the fans hidden because she thinks Aunt Alice would ban them," Nate confided.

"Can I see the electrical clothes washer? I did the tablecloth in the sink here 'cause I never even heard of such a thing."

Nate walked Allie to the pantry and lifted her up for a look at the inside of the washer.

"There's no light in here. Where do you get the electricity?" she said.

Nate reached behind the machine and revealed a long, coiled electrical cord with a plug on the end.

"You run the cord into the kitchen and plug it into a light sconce. But you shouldn't because you're too young. Clothes washers are very dangerous machines," Nate cautioned.

"Pshaw. More dangerous than a bull or a kicking mule?"

"I don't know about that, but grown women get killed washing clothes every day of the week. They're careless and get their sleeves caught in the ringer and their arms are ripped off before anyone hears their screams and unplugs the machine. So stay away."

Allie stared at Nate for a few seconds, a smile spreading across her face. "I solemnly swear I will not use this electric clothes washer, if you will make me electricity toast with butter and jam."

Nate agreed happily. They folded the tablecloth, stacked the encyclopedias temporarily in a corner, plugged in the toaster, sliced half a loaf of bread, and started cooking.

"Allie, do you know who fed the furnace?"

"It was like this. When we got back from shopping— and that was fine, let me tell you. Those stores are so big and—"

"The furnace?"

"Well, Aunt Alice and Cousin Deborah were tuckered out when we got back, and it was getting cold, so Aunt Alice asked me to go wake up Marina and Bea and have them stoke the fire like Aunt Alice said. Well, I went upstairs, but they both were sleeping and sounding terrible sick, breathing bad, so I decided to do it myself."

"Do you have a coal furnace in Georgia?"

"Shoot no," she said, wiping apple preserves from the corner of her mouth. "I figured it out myself—that's what my pa always told me to do. He always lets me take care of things."

"There are certain jobs a man should do himself."

"Not if he's got children, silly. That's what children are for."

"But . . . you mean there are more of you back home?"

"No, it's just me and Pa. But I'm all the help he needs," Allie said proudly.

Nate stared and thought. She really was hungry, judging by the way she ripped into the toast. He guessed that her trip from Georgia had been long, tiring, and skimpy on meals.

"Let me make you a real sandwich, okay?" he asked.

She smiled and nodded her head approvingly.

15

Christmas Eve Day began brilliantly. The sun glistened on newly fallen snow. Nate rose early to tend the furnace but wasn't needed.

"Everything back to normal," Marina said as she busied herself in the kitchen. "Bea shovel the ashes and add coal long time ago. Don't you feel heat up there?"

"I do; it is toasty warm. I should have noticed."

"Now you here, maybe you want some cocoa before breakfast?"

Nate smiled and rubbed his stomach in a big circle. He went to get milk, but the cook blocked his path to the icebox.

"Everything normal now. You sit. I cook."

"Caterwauling corn fritters!" Allie exclaimed as she burst through the door. "My pa says, 'Watch out for the shy, quiet types 'cause still waters run deep.' Oh boy! Is that ever true with *you*, Cousin."

"Of course I'm deep. I've seen things you can't even guess at," he said, half teasing her.

"Want to bet? I know you're friends with the most famous *murderer* in the city!"

Marina dropped a pot. Milk splashed across the floor, but she didn't move an inch.

"Murderer! Why you say Nate knows murderer?"

"I didn't say it, a newspaper did." Allie whipped the morning's *Herald* from behind her back to reveal a mug shot of Ace, frowning, next to a publicity photo of Houdini, smiling. Nate snatched the paper from her hands.

Scanning the page, he saw the incriminating words:

Nathaniel Fuller, previously linked to both Houdini and criminal violence in these pages, is a known associate of Winchell. Mr. Fuller, previously a student at St. Paul's School, resides at 18 East Fifty-third Street—the home of his great-aunt, Alice Ludlow. Mrs. Ludlow is the widow of Arthur Ludlow, a merchant prominent for four decades in our city . . .

There was more, but Nate stopped because Marina was breathing rapidly on the back of his neck.

"It's a mistake, Marina. All a mistake," he said, and repeated it until the cook calmed down. The noise had brought Bea into the room from the pantry. When Marina's daughter asked what was wrong, it caused an avalanche of words in Polish. At least that gave Nate a second to warn Allie.

"It's all a mistake," he whispered fiercely, his eyebrows arched painfully high. "Don't say any more. They're terrified as it is."

Fortunately, Allie complied. While Nate worked to settle the agitated help, she located a bucket and sponge to clean up the spilled milk. When Marina calmed down enough to realize that her employer's niece was on her knees swabbing the floor, she lifted Allie up, scolded her, and insisted that the children go to the dining room to wait for breakfast to be served.

Nate was happy to oblige. He walked Allie out with a hand firmly against her spine.

"Great balls of cotton, I got the message!" Allie protested loudly.

Nate shushed her with a finger to his lips.

"All right, I won't scare them again," she said in an exaggerated whisper. "But what are you going to tell Aunt Alice? She's not going to like being in the papers."

Nate moaned silently. His great-aunt was a firm believer that the family's private life should stay private.

"She's not going to know about it unless *you* tell her."

Allie looked back wide-eyed.

"I will tell her . . . somebody will . . . at the right time. Aunt Alice doesn't read newspapers," he said, regaining his confidence, "so there's no reason to stick one in her face first thing in the morning."

"Is your friend really the bad egg they say—"

"It's a complete, absolute, total frame-up!"

"You're sure about that?" she asked softly.

"I'm sure. Houdini's sure. Every sane person is sure."

"That's a relief, 'cause I hate to think that I'm best friends with a boy who can't tell a crazy person from a boiled turnip."

"How could you think he's guilty? He bought you lunch!" Nate said in a wounded tone.

"He *was* kind of strange with that electric chair, wasn't he?"

Nate turned away from Allie to concentrate on the *Herald*'s headlines. Houdini was right. It hadn't stayed secret for long:

FIFTH AVENUE SLASHER HOUDINI'S PUPIL?
WILL HOUDINI BREAK SLASHER OUT OF JAIL?
MAN OF MYSTERY DEFENDS BLOODY GHOUL!
WHO TAUGHT WINCHELL THE ART OF SILENT
BREAKING AND ENTERING?

Reading further, Nate saw that Houdini was quoted in the article:

"Miles, Dewey and Davis have engaged a top detective firm to investigate my employee's claim of innocence," the world-renowned entertainer told this reporter. "No effort, or expense, will be spared in getting to the truth, but I shall not personally be involved. I shall rely solely upon their skills."

The writer then made a ridiculous assertion:

The escapologist/magician chilled this reporter's blood by hinting that he possessed supernatural powers. "When young Mr. Winchell is exonerated, I will not have it said that Houdini bewitched the district attorney or controlled the minds of jurors," Houdini said. "The notion that I have such abilities is pure flapdoodle, but rumors will abound nonetheless if I am involved in his defense."

Hinted he had supernatural powers? Houdini said outrightly that was flapdoodle. But maybe he was happy to serve as a distraction.

Before Nate got back to the part mentioning his link to Ace, the phone rang.

Allie began jumping up and down. "I bet you that's Houdini. I bet you it's about Ace. You've just got to let me come with you today," she pleaded, dragging at Nate's sleeve. "Ace is my friend, too. You said so yourself."

"Hello, this is Longacre 6533," he said, praying that it wasn't a reporter at the other end of the line.

"We are found out, my friend!" Houdini bellowed.

"Boy, do I ever know that."

"Since secrecy is no longer possible, will you visit Ace with me this Christmas Eve morn? I have food Mrs. Houdini insists that I deliver."

"I'll be at the door waiting," Nate said. After hanging up, he decided it was time to inform his mother that his family was in the news—again.

16

"Publicity is my lifeblood; privacy is your great-aunt's. She understands?" Houdini asked skeptically.

Once again, they were heading downtown in Frankie Bonamino's car.

"She will . . . after my mother explains."

"Your great-aunt is a formidable lady. You shouldn't deceive her."

"I haven't! I just didn't tell her anything before I left."

"Let us hope your mother puts Ace's predicament in the best light before anything untoward happens."

"Like a reporter calling?"

Houdini waved a hand through the air. "That possibility has been dealt with. I was thinking of your cousin innocently blurting out something that would alarm your aunt Alice."

"My cousin? How do you know about my cousin?" Nate asked.

"Never ask me to divulge my secrets, Nate."

"Is dealing with the press a secret?" Nate asked after a thoughtful silence.

"Not at all. You know that Houdini is *always* news. But Houdini linked to a murder, that is a one hundred percent circulation booster."

"But won't reporters follow us everywhere now?"

"Of course not. Shadowing us is a dreary, uncomfortable task. And entirely unnecessary since I've promised that I will provide the reporters sensational copy every day about our progress."

"And you'll do that every day?"

"I already have. I typed a summary of today's activities this morning. Mrs. Houdini will call it in to the evening papers an hour or so before their deadlines," Houdini said, glowing with a satisfaction that seemed to warm Frankie's car as he negotiated the thick holiday traffic.

"Yes. We need some breathing room to prove Ace innocent and return him to my workshop. How else can I perfect my death-defying . . . audience-mystifying . . . Water Torture Escape?"

Judging from the lightness of Houdini's tone, Nate guessed this might be the first time Houdini had looked forward to resuming his career since his mother's death.

"That's the spirit," said Frankie. "Everything is going to work out just fine."

The mood darkened as they approached the intersection of White and Lafayette streets, where the Halls of Justice dominated the skyline. New York City's main prison was nicknamed the Tombs because the massive stone building resembled an Egyptian mausoleum. Nate shuddered at the sight of it, knowing that hundreds of vicious career criminals were housed inside—and that some of them were probably nervous about sharing the place with the purported Fifth Avenue Slasher.

"We're meeting Captain Root," Houdini told an officer at the visitors' desk.

"There's been a change of plan." An authoritative middle-aged woman approached them. Her graying hair was wrapped into a tight bun; a stiffly starched shirt topped her ebony-black floor-length skirt. The woman's smile was appealing, but Nate found her gait curiously stiff, almost military.

"Captain Root is taking a week's leave. He asked me to do what I can for you, given the circumstances." She lowered her voice near the end of her statement.

"By Jove! It's Police Matron Goodwin," Houdini said.

"*Detective* Goodwin," she said.

"Detective?" Houdini asked.

"As of last week, sir."

"Will wonders never cease?" Houdini said, then quickly corrected himself. "No, no, no. It's *not* a wonder.

It's high time. Nate Fuller, meet *Detective* Isabella Goodwin."

"I knew the department had police matrons, but not women detectives," Nate said.

"It didn't. Not before last week. I started as a matron in '96, and now I am the first woman detective on the force."

"Possibly the world's first," Houdini noted.

"And I earned it—on the square. I worked the Bowery undercover these last three years."

"Then you're the cop to help us," Nate said excitedly. Houdini frowned at the slang *cop*, but Detective Goodwin took no offense.

"I'm the cop indeed. Should we talk with the prisoner now? I reserved an interrogation room."

"What commendable foresight," Houdini said.

"I'll have the prisoner brought up then."

Nate frowned. Ace no longer had a name, he was just "the prisoner."

"Am I glad to see you!" Ace said minutes later, clanking into the interview room. The shackles on his ankles made walking difficult; painful, too, judging by his grimace.

Houdini embraced the assistant who had grown taller than his employer during the past several months. Ace couldn't return the hug. Not with handcuffs around his wrists.

"Can't you take those off?" Nate asked Detective Goodwin after Ace was seated at a table in the bare room.

"Not in a public room like this, young man. I'd lose my shield if someone found him unshackled."

"If I was Houdini, I'd already have the cuffs on the lady copper and be on my way home," Ace said.

"But then you would be a fugitive," Houdini said. "When Nate and I and Detective Goodwin find the culprit, your shackles will fall away forever."

"Ouch!" said Detective Goodwin. "The captain 'asked' me to do what I could, but on the q.t. Officially, I am just extending a courtesy to Mr. Houdini, a good friend of the department."

"Point taken," Houdini said graciously. "Ace, you'd better do all you can to help yourself—beginning now."

"Whatever I can," Ace said. Holding out his bound hands, he raised an eyebrow and said, "But I'm not sure that will amount to much."

"Start with your alibi."

"I don't have one," Ace said sadly. "I told Mr. Miles that."

"I know," Houdini said, wrapping his hand around Ace's forearm. "We need to hear for ourselves. Nate will take notes, if you don't mind."

Ace looked downward and composed himself before resuming.

"It was payday, and I was dog tired. We'd worked sixteen hours straight on the water-torture cell. So when I got home, my ma took the kids to the baths on Allen Street while I got a nap."

"A bath every payday then?" Detective Goodwin asked.

"Like clockwork."

"Did they come home for dinner, or did you meet them somewhere?" Houdini asked.

Ace laughed and looked about sheepishly when no one else joined in.

"You pay good, Houdini, but not good enough to take a bunch of kids out to dinner. Besides, I'm putting away a little every week to get deposit money for a new apartment . . . in a better neighborhood. Maybe even Brooklyn."

"Just like myself at your age," Houdini said.

"After the little ones were under the covers, I took one of the magic books you loaned me and read it on the subway to the Bronx and back."

"The subway, where you can get solitude, electric light, and heat for a nickel. I would have done the same when I was your age, if the subway had been built," Houdini said.

"Somebody must have seen you?" Nate coaxed.

"I don't think so. There weren't many people traveling that late. Besides, I sit in the last car."

"And you had a book hiding your face," Houdini added.

"It looks bad for me, doesn't it, boss?"

Nate wanted to cheer Ace up, tell him they had already

proved the state's witnesses were lying. But they hadn't done that. They only had suspicions, not proof.

"I cannot tell you a path of roses lies ahead," Houdini admitted. "But we've only just begun."

"And we won't give up until we get you out of here," Nate added with an emphatic bang on the table.

"Have you ever had any dustups with Honest Bill Gates?" Detective Goodwin asked.

I wonder what she knows, Nate asked himself, making a note for his case file. *Or is she just being logical?*

"Chee no! Mr. Miles read me his statement. I could hardly believe my ears."

"Do you know him at all?" Houdini asked.

Ace dropped his head and muttered forlornly to himself. He spread his hands as far apart as the cuffs would allow and tugged hard, as if hoping they would fall off.

"No more than to pass by and say 'Hi, how's it going?' But that's like a thousand people in the neighborhood. Sure I've bought clothes at his place, but I always dealt with one of his flunky clerks."

"Like his redheaded son?" Nate asked, resisting the temptation to call him the "shifty, suspicious-acting son."

"Probably I talked with him," Ace said after some thought. "He doesn't make much of an impression, I guess."

"Nate, you're getting all this?" Houdini asked.

Nate nodded yes, his mind racing with questions while his pencil raced across the journal pages.

"Have you—or has anyone in your family—ever run afoul of Max Eastman?"

"Eastman? Hully Gee! You think he's framing me?"

"We're not excluding anyone yet," Houdini said as he circled the table and put his hands on Ace's shoulders. Until then, Detective Goodwin had been sitting passively, hands folded in her lap. She wagged a finger and pointed Houdini back to his chair.

"Be truthful, son. Did you ever cross Eastman?" the woman detective asked.

"I was young, but not stupid. Crossing Mad Max is suicide."

"What is the family debt you were working off?" Nate asked.

"Huh?" Ace asked.

"Max Eastman implied that your family owed a debt to Crazy Butch," Nate explained. "What was it?"

"I don't have a clue," Ace said, amazement filling his face.

"That's what we're here for, my boy," Houdini said confidently. "To find the clues, get the answers, and exonerate you."

"You think so? I really hope I get out of this place."

"Don't worry. Finding the real murderer won't be easy," Nate said, "but we'll do it."

Nate and Houdini smiled, hoping to reassure their imprisoned friend. Surprisingly, Detective Goodwin laughed loudly. "Finding a murderer on the Bowery is no great feat, young man. Finding the murderer you're after is a horse of a different color."

"Excuse me, let's return to the subject of cake," Houdini said. "I have one from Mrs. Houdini and another from Mrs. Bonamino. Which would you like first, Ace?"

17

A guard returned Ace to his cell, and a quiet trio made their way toward the building's exit. Houdini kicked at an imaginary obstacle in his path.

"I had hoped Ace could shed some light on this mystery," he said distractedly.

"I forgot to ask Ace what his cell mate is like," Nate said. "And if his mattress is infested with bedbugs."

"I can't help with your investigations, but I can give you some peace of mind there," Detective Goodwin said. "The city doesn't want any outbreaks of infection in the Tombs. Everything is spick-and-span as can be."

"And Ace's cell mate?"

"He doesn't have one. I heard a rumor his life was threatened. Since all the department nobs are away, I took it upon myself to have the boy put in solitary."

"Bless you, Detective," Houdini said.

At the visitors' entrance, Detective Goodwin wished Nate and Houdini luck and walked toward her office at Police Headquarters, leaning into the arctic wind.

"It's not far to Ace's flat. We should call on his family today," Houdini said as they piled into Mr. Bonamino's car.

"It's rotten that Ace is going to spend Christmas in jail," Nate observed, causing Frankie to agree in a torrent of English and Italian.

"Gentlemen!" Houdini interrupted. "Trust me! Being alone on Christmas Day will not be the *worst* thing that has ever befallen our friend. And he will have visitors bearing gifts."

When the car reached Rivington Street, Houdini insisted that their chauffeur drop them off and return home to prepare for the upcoming festivities.

As they waved goodbye, increasingly frigid winds knifed through Nate's heavy woolen coat. Looking up and down the busy street, he was shocked to see how very few Lower East Side residents had winter coats or boots. He shivered to think about how cold they must feel.

After making a four-flight climb, Houdini rapped loudly on the Winchells' front door, prompting a stampede of footsteps. When the door swung open, three eager children recognized their guest instantly and jostled each other to get closest to him.

"We are sorry to arrive unannounced," Houdini said. "How are you holding up, Mrs. Winchell?"

"Best I can—having birthed and raised a bloodthirsty killer," she answered. Her tone was angry, but her eyes were sad, and very red from lack of sleep or crying. "And yourselves?"

"Er . . . quite fine," Nate replied uncertainly.

"Courage, ma'am! You *can't* believe that Ace is guilty," Houdini said.

"There's nothing men won't do, that's all I know. It's a man what gave me all this," she said, waving an arm at her pitiable surroundings.

The furniture was decrepit, the paint was peeling, the walls were undecorated except for stains and gouges, and the children were dressed in frayed and dirty clothing. To make matters worse, it was cold—almost as cold as the street. No wonder Ace rode the subway at night to read.

"I'm at sea," Houdini said. "Your son has been bringing home an honestly earned pay packet for nearly five years. His future in my organization is, in all modesty, bright. What makes you think he would turn to crime now?"

Or torture? Nate wondered. A mother should defend her son with her last gasp; his mother would. Aunt Alice would.

"Are you telling me he didn't do it?" Ace's mother sounded shocked.

"That's right, and we already know who did it!" Nate burst out.

"Let's not get ahead of ourselves, Nate," Houdini warned. "However, Mrs. Winchell, I can assure you—I can swear—that Ace had *nothing* to do with the grotesque crime."

"But . . ." she asked softly.

"One hundred percent innocent," Houdini insisted, his penetrating blue eyes locked on the poor woman.

She was quiet for a moment, then wailed and fell to the floor. Houdini and Nate both instinctively knelt beside Mrs. Winchell to comfort her.

Her small children shrank back toward the corners of the room. Nate guessed this wasn't the first time they had seen this behavior.

Ace's mother sobbed for minutes. When she began running out of steam, they helped her up to a chair. Finally stanching the tears, she thanked Houdini and Nate, then cursed the police and cursed herself for believing them.

Nate realized that Mrs. Winchell and her son shared the same physical features—high cheekbones, elongated noses, and light brown hair.

"The police told you that Ace was guilty?" Houdini suggested.

"Two stinking, turd-faced detectives . . . they came the night Ace was arrested," she said with difficulty. Her throat and nose were so full of mucus the woman was barely understandable. Houdini gave her a handkerchief and convinced her to use it.

"They said, 'We got evidence to send him and your whole family to the electric chair, if we like.' Those were the very words they said to me, just finding out my boy was in jail."

Houdini shook his head sadly.

"Then they said they were going to look around, see if the rest of the loot was here . . . or the knife. So they searched and searched. Tore the place apart, but they didn't find nothing."

"Because there was nothing to find, of course," Nate said.

"That's not how *they* looked at it. They gathered around and pitched in on me. Asked me thousands of questions. Accused me of hiding the loot and washing his bloody clothes. Said they were going to put me away. Leave my kids with no mother, they said. God preserve me!"

"Convinced finally that you weren't shielding your son, they left," Houdini prompted. "Perhaps they apologized?"

"Them? May them two mugs eat nothing but stones and dirt in the gutter—now that you tell me my boy is clean. The filth! May those two never see the sun shine again." She turned away jerkily and spat on the floor.

Nate was about to ask a question when Houdini touched a finger to his lips.

"Ma," a girl about Allie's age whispered, "can we go out?"

"Where to? You'll freeze your arses off!"

The child began to slink away when Houdini—on his feet, snapping his fingers, and smiling—dashed to pick her up and sit her on a corner of the table.

"You're Meg, aren't you?" he asked.

"I am," she said with amazement as Houdini beckoned her brother and other sister to the table.

Nate was stunned that Houdini knew the child's name.

"Your mother is right. It's far too cold to play outside. And it could be worth your while to stay here. Let me show you."

Houdini fished around inside his coat very obviously. Nate guessed that he must be retrieving something from his hanky-panky pocket.

"Here we are!" Houdini said as he slapped a small tin bowl on the tabletop. He lifted it between two fingers to reveal a nearly identical bowl beneath the first. He repeated the motion, ending with three small bowls lined up before Ace's sister.

"Now let me see what else I have . . . Here we are. Look at this tiny green rubber ball. Let's play a game," Houdini said as he twirled the ball between thumb and index finger. "Meg, I want you to turn those bowls over and look inside them." When she obeyed, he instructed her to hold each one in her hands, to feel inside the bowl and make certain each was empty.

"They are," she said meekly.

"Excellent! Then I will put this green rubber ball under the middle bowl. All right? Now I will shuffle all three bowls—watch very closely—and you tell where the ball is hiding. Would you like to try?"

Meg agreed to play. Her brother and sister stood behind, watching.

Then Houdini moved the bowls very slowly, and only one at a time, making it impossible for Ace's sister to lose track of where the ball was hidden. He stopped.

"All right, Meg, where is the ball? Go ahead, pick up the bowl it's hiding under," Houdini said.

She picked up a bowl and gasped. A shiny silver dollar, not the green ball, was under the bowl.

"How on earth did that get there?" Houdini said. He scratched his head as if completely confused.

"Well, finders keepers is only fair," he said, and pressed the silver dollar into her hand.

"Mr. Houdini, that girl has never had more than a nickel in her life. You can't be giving her that," Mrs. Winchell said.

"But the coin is not mine. Your daughter found it, so it should be hers. Let me see if young Gerald has better luck finding the ball."

Houdini played the game with Ace's younger brother and achieved the same result somehow. The little green ball wasn't under the bowl. But sure enough, a silver dollar was. And it happened a third time with the youngest child, Elizabeth.

"I guess I've gotten rusty," Houdini said in mock seriousness.

Now the kids really wanted to go out, their newly found fortunes in hand. Mrs. Winchell exchanged each of the silver dollars for a five-cent piece and let them leave. Surprisingly, they were nearly as happy to have a nickel in hand as a dollar.

"Is there anything else?" Houdini asked. "About the police visit?"

"There was. And I want you to know why I was so hard-hearted about my boy. Those dicks, they brung out a book of pictures . . . photographs."

"Photographs?" Nate asked.

"They called them crime scene pictures," she said, and shuddered visibly. "I remember you from last summer. My boy saved your life."

"I intend to return the favor."

"They made me look at them horrible pictures. Blood everywhere. Cuts all over the poor soul's body. Throat sliced ear to ear. And the dicks *swore* they had witnesses and evidence and some cigars . . . and it all proved that my boy did the burglary and robbery and murder."

She paused again, seeming deep in thought.

"But I knew it was a lie. *I knew*, in my heart, I knew *my* boy couldn't do nothing like that . . . no matter what kind of lying, cheating piece of filth his father was. God save me, I got to get back to my work," she said, pointing to a round galvanized tub filled with wet laundry. Her red hands, cracked and sore-looking, appeared far too pained to rub pounds of sopping wet cotton against a washboard.

But Nate knew that she would do just that. And then she would iron and fold the hundreds of garments she had washed. She had been doing that seven days a week since before Ace had been born.

"We've taken far too much of your time, but there is one more thing I need to discuss," Houdini said. "Nate, I fear Mr. Bonamino must think we've abandoned him. Please tell him I will be down in a moment."

Knowing their driver had long since left, Nate assumed that this was Houdini's code for "I need to speak with Ace's mother alone." Nate nodded at Houdini, then said goodbye and made for the door. Before exiting, he turned and looked Mrs. Winchell in the eye. "Don't you worry, ma'am. Ace is nearly as good as home right now."

He left, and was joined by Houdini at the foot of the stairs a few minutes later.

"I couldn't find Frankie Bonamino," Nate said wryly.

"That's right, I completely forgot that he went home," Houdini joked. "Let's take the El train to Cooper Square and find a taxi home from there."

"You know, Mrs. Winchell may need help carrying all the food and presents she buys with the money you just gave her."

"Fear not, partner. She was fetching a neighbor as I left. And for the record, I merely delivered Ace's Christmas bonus. It may as well do some good . . ."

Houdini's sentence trailed off as he pulled open the front door and faced a stranger glaring at them on the building's stoop.

18

Get the straight dope for once, why don't you? Talk with *me!*"

The challenge came from the most extraordinarily dressed man Nate had ever seen. Beneath a fur overcoat, he wore a brilliant red and green windowpane-check suit and a vest of two-inch red and green vertical stripes. A lavender-colored necktie accentuated purple facial scars that zigzagged and intersected like rivers on a map. A pearl gray derby tilted to the right side of his head under-scored his aggressive posture—hands on hips, hips thrusting forward.

His female companion was no less extraordinary. She

wore a checked jacket, tightly cinched at the waist, and a flame red dress. Two foot-long multicolored bird feathers jutted at opposing angles from her hat. Even at a distance, Nate could see that powder and rouge hid her skin completely from the winter afternoon sun.

"That's what we're after, the straight story," Houdini said. "But this is no day for a sidewalk chat."

"Ain't that the truth," the colorful stranger replied casually. "Let me buy you a drink at me saloon."

"Sorry, we're teetotalers."

"Chee! That's goin' around like the influenza. Terrible for business." He then suggested a restaurant on the Bowery. Houdini agreed and let the two strangers lead the way. It was too short a distance to hire a cab, but it proved a long walk in the frigid weather. And their progress was slowed painfully by the woman's unsteady gait; her slip-on red heels were not designed for walking.

Heads turned when the group walked in, but nobody was looking at Houdini or Nate. Two uniformed policemen in a booth tipped their caps respectfully and resumed their conversation.

"Clothes make the man! And blue and brass got no class," the stranger said very loudly. The police pretended not to have heard him.

Judging from his breezy, confident manner, and the gaudy jewelry he and his companion wore, Nate deduced that the man was well known to be on the wrong side of the law. This must have been Crazy Butch or Kid Twist. Nate figured a person called Louie the Lump had to be fat.

"You obviously know who I am," Houdini said while helping the woman into her chair. "Nate is a colleague."

"I'm Butch McGurk. This is me bundle, Iris."

"Pleased to meecha," she said with an eye-fluttering smile.

"Iris, I couldn't fail to notice that you are carrying a small-caliber revolver inside your coat," Houdini said with a smile.

"Yeh," she challenged. "So?"

"These times," Crazy Butch McGurk said, clicking his tongue a few times. "That pain-in-the-rear-end Sullivan fella."

"You mean Senator Sullivan's new gun-control law? That makes carrying concealed firearms in New York illegal?" Nate asked, following Houdini's lead.

"That's the one, kiddo," Butch replied. "If some cop rousts me and finds a gat, I'm outta the picture—up the river for God knows how long."

"So Iris carries your gun because she can't be searched by a policeman," Houdini surmised.

Butch grinned through tobacco-colored teeth.

"There *are* women policemen, you know," Nate said.

"She's willin' to run that risk, ain't you, Iris?"

"Anything for my man," Iris said sincerely.

"Only a coward would force his—" the boy muttered.

"Nate! Time and place?" Houdini cautioned.

"Chee! Let's not get off on the bad foot here, okay, kiddo?" Butch extended a hand for Nate to shake.

"It's not my place to criticize," Nate admitted while pumping it.

"Good grip for a puny one," Butch said. "Anyway, a dozen eyes and ears told me you two are runnin' around asking questions, stirring people up."

"And if that is the case?" Houdini asked.

The gangster's good humor evaporated as his eyes tried to bore a hole through Houdini's forehead.

"Maybe you didn't hear me. I'm Butch McGurk."

"We heard you perfectly well," Houdini said.

"Do you know what that means?" he asked, his voice more angry with each word.

"We're all ears," Houdini said.

"You think you're funny, don't you?" Butch said menacingly. He took a cigar from his coat pocket, rolled it on the table, bit the end off, and lit it very slowly. After taking a few leisurely puffs, he continued. "You *waltz* into my territory. You *bother* people in their own store. You ask questions about things that aren't *none* of your business. Without *my* permission!"

"Max said you *share* the territory with Twist and Lump," Houdini said. "You could do a vaudeville act with those names. I can see it in lights: 'The Comic Stylings of Twist, Lump, and McGurk.' "

"Damn that Max," Crazy Butch said, and spat on the

floor to show contempt for his old boss, not even trying to hit one of the restaurant's numerous spittoons. "But that's neither here nor there. The point is, not even the chief of police comes to my territory asking questions without gettin' a high sign from me first. Who do you think you are?" he yelled.

"Just two people trying to help a friend," Houdini said.

"Yeah, I heard about your friend."

"But you *knew* him," Houdini said. "Ace worked for you."

Butch puffed and painstakingly blew smoke rings. Nate glanced at Iris, who seemed perfectly content to stare at street traffic through the restaurant's front window. Two waiters hovered a short distance from the table—ready to offer service the instant Crazy Butch wanted it. The uniformed policemen had left, their meals uneaten. If Butch went crazy on a couple of tourists that day, they didn't want to be the cops on the scene.

"If the kid was still with *me*, he wouldn't have this bother."

"I think the death penalty is more than a 'bother,'" Nate protested.

"Didn't I tell you to watch that lip, kid?"

"How would you have prevented Ace's arrest?" Houdini asked. "Because Gates wouldn't have fingered Ace without your blessing? Or because Ace wouldn't have been housebreaking if he worked for you?"

"Take your pick," Butch said smugly.

"Or possibly the reverse?" Nate asked.

"Huh?"

"Maybe Honest Bill fingered Ace with evidence *you* gave him," Nate said. "And the police arrested Ace because *you* told them he was guilty."

Crazy Butch snapped his fingers; both waiters ran to the table.

"Hey, you mugs, at least put some coffee and some bread on the table," the gangster said, ignoring Nate.

"Don't be cross with my colleague for suggesting that you framed Ace," Houdini said. "We're convinced that he was framed. And you've implied that you have absolute power in your neighborhood."

"You dopes are ignorant. So I'm going to school you," Butch said in measured tones. "People can't survive in this city without protection. People like you—that live in uptown mansions—they got the mayor and the governor and the president for friends."

The gangster paused to appreciate his growing cigar ash.

"People here on the Bowery, the only friend they got is me. The only square deal they get is from me. They got nothing without my help."

"You haven't been much help to Ace's family. They really have nothing," Nate said. "I guess the family debt they owed you was never paid off."

For a long moment, Butch looked ready to explode. Then calm spread across his face. "You know the old saying: Fool me once, shame on you. Fool me twice, shame on me?" he asked.

"Of course," Houdini said.

"Well, some people don't deserve nothing. Old Lady Winchell and her brood should starve and rot."

"Heavens, man, she's the mother of small children. She feeds them by scrubbing underwear in a cold-water tenement. What could *she* have done to you?" Houdini asked.

Without saying another word, Crazy Butch crushed his burning cigar on the tablecloth, peeled several dollar bills from a roll, threw them on the table, then turned and walked toward the door. Iris casually followed, as if that was the way most meals ended. Houdini and Nate sat in silence until they exited.

"Is that the motive?" Nate asked. "Butch pinned the murder on Ace because Butch hates Ace's mother?"

"He made that a logical conclusion to draw," Houdini said.

The restaurant's front door flew open again with a crash. Butch marched directly back to their table and glared down. "You're thinking there was something between me and the kid's mother, ain't you?"

There was spittle in the corners of the gangster's mouth. His cheeks were flushed. His hands were balled into fists.

"Well, there was. Years ago I was sweet on her. But she took up with a smooth-talking lowlife called Bugsy

Winchell. Good for her. Until Winchell blew town and left her broke."

Houdini nodded appreciatively, encouraging Crazy Butch.

"Didn't I throw her bucks now and then? Didn't I give her whelp the chance to be my right-hand man? And didn't he bite the hand what fed him? Gets a job and shows me his back."

"This all sounds like motive for revenge," Houdini observed.

"Don't be chumps, poking around in business that ain't yours. Go back uptown and forget about that kid while you still can."

"We cannot!" Houdini insisted.

"Why? The kid's a goner."

"And you had nothing to do with that?"

"Look, I'll swear to you on a stack of Bibles or on my mother's grave or whatever you like: I never saw that cigar case. I got nothing to do with it. If Honest Bill says that kid sold it to him, Bill's telling the truth."

"And you never mentioned Ace to Honest Bill?"

"Never! I ain't thought about that kid in years."

"Or his mother?" Nate asked.

"That's enough!" he said, pounding the table. "Beat it. And you won't come back here if you're as smart as you think you are."

They watched him turn and stalk out a second time.

"A most dramatic fellow," Houdini eventually commented. "I believe we've done all that we can this day, don't you?"

"We could order," Nate said with the waiters glowering at him. "I'm famished."

Houdini nodded. "I could eat." Leaning toward Nate, he whispered, "But not here."

19

Houdini pushed his chair away from the table and moaned an *aaah* of thorough satisfaction; Nate followed suit. They had devoured six-inch-high pastrami sandwiches, a mountain of coleslaw, and no telling how many pickles. All washed down with egg creams.

"Am I correct? Is Katz's Delicatessen the *only* place to eat below Fourteenth Street?" Houdini asked.

"I'll say it is," Nate agreed, not wanting to contradict the showman or reveal his lack of worldly experience. Katz's on Houston Street was actually the first kosher eatery Nate had ever visited. And it was the first time he had tasted seasoned smoked beef quite like pastrami. But that didn't mean it wasn't the best.

"Home then," Houdini said.

"Maybe we should split up now. I need to buy another present," Nate said as Allie popped back into his mind.

"Allow me to accompany you? I have excellent taste. World-renowned," Houdini replied.

Nate couldn't refuse, so after Houdini settled the bill and hailed a cab, they traveled north.

The ride reminded Nate that it really was Christmastime.

Salvation Army Santas, wreath sellers, and roasted-chestnut vendors were everywhere, even though most of the shoppers had gone home already. The taxi stopped for one of the city's new electric traffic lights at East Twenty-third Street and Madison. On the corner, a sandwich-board man's sign read, TOM'S MADISON SQUARE DEAL: FOUR-COURSE CHRISTMAS TURKEY OR GOOSE DINNER, ONLY 25¢.

When the cab arrived at Macy's main entrance, Houdini unveiled a change of plan. "I intend to spread some cheer at the Magicians' Society—it's quite near—while you shop. I should not influence a personal decision. But take my card and present it to Mr. Klein or Mr. Osgood. I'll be here when you're finished."

Doing just as he was told worked like magic. Mr. Klein eagerly determined that the present was for a ten-year-old girl who needed practically everything and sent three clerks to work. They returned minutes later with a smiling dog doll called Puppy Pippin, a pair of fur-lined gloves, and a brooch with a sparkly emerald-colored stone.

"Gosh, I'm not sure which she'd like best," Nate said, feeling overwhelmed.

"I recommend all three," Mr. Klein suggested.

"All three! I'm not sure I have enough for one of them."

"Certainly they are on the Houdinis' account," Mr. Klein said, brushing away Nate's concern with a wave of his hand that also caused the clerks to scurry off. Nate said that he could not let Houdini pay for his purchases, but the forceful Mr. Klein insisted that that was not his concern—satisfying the Houdinis was.

"If any of the items fail to suit, simply return them at your leisure," he said, opening the main door minutes later as Nate left with all three elegantly wrapped and topped with colorful bows and ribbons. As promised, Houdini was waiting in the same cab that had brought them uptown.

"They wouldn't let me pay for anything," Nate said.

"Would you expect anything less of Houdini? It's Christmas after all," the magician replied.

"I'd be happy to accept one—as your present to me— but three? I have to pay you back."

"And you will if you like. Never let it be said Houdini makes his friends feel guilty. But for the moment, be done with it. Agreed?"

"Agreed," Nate said, feeling better. "And thank you very much."

Nate looked at the presents and was troubled by them. Images of Ace's family flooded his mind. A picture of Ace in a jail cell followed. "Poor Ace," he said involuntarily.

"Trouble shared is trouble halved, my friend. With so many friends working on Ace's behalf, his troubles are whittled away to nothing. Practically nothing."

"I know, but it's hard to pretend that spending Christmas in a jail cell is—"

"Enough, my young friend. We did not put him there, but we will get him out!" Houdini promised.

"Is it possible that you and Mrs. Houdini could visit us tomorrow, since we're taking time out from our investigation? My mother would love that."

"As would we. But we've already made plans to do hospital visits. It's the least I can do, considering my good fortune in life."

Nate knew that Houdini often spent holidays entertaining sick children, orphaned children—the entertainer's gift to those who couldn't attend theaters or even watch his free public exhibitions. Houdini had once told Nate that if one hundred thousand people showed up in Boston or San Francisco to watch him jump from a bridge in handcuffs and leg-irons, not one of the one hundred thousand spectators was a child with infantile paralysis or tuberculosis. Houdini said Christmas should be *their* day.

"Bess had already lined up five shows before I left this morning," Houdini continued. "With an hour of magic and mystery at each stop and all the travel, I'll be doing tricks with cards and coins and handkerchiefs from dawn till midnight," he said gleefully.

"I'd love to see that," Nate said, "but so would Ace and his—"

"Look, you come home to a celebration!" Houdini interrupted as the cab rolled to a stop on Nate's street.

"You're right," Nate said, surprised to see that the house was ablaze with light—an extravagance Aunt Alice never tolerated.

"Enjoy it, because there will be enough to do soon enough," Houdini said as he opened the door to let Nate out. "Merry Christmas to all."

"The same to you and Mrs. Houdini," Nate said as the cab sputtered away. He climbed the stairs and heard a voice singing as he entered the house. It was Allie, trying to carry "Hark! The Herald Angels Sing" by herself.

Allie is a game one, he thought while stashing her presents in the ornamental antique sideboard Aunt Alice positioned opposite the coat pegs.

"Well, young man, I discovered what urgent business prompted you to abandon your studies, your household duties, and *your family* on Christmas Eve," his great-aunt said, entering the parlor doorway.

"That's good," he replied guardedly. "And I'm glad that you sound so much better. Totally cured."

"Do not attempt to divert me, Nephew. I know that you and that vaudevillian have been consorting with criminals all day."

"I'm just trying to help a friend."

The elderly woman breathed deeply, then walked over to Nate and extended her bent elbow. "Take my arm, Nathaniel. Clearly, it is as fruitless to argue with you as it is to argue with any man."

Before he could really appreciate being referred to as a man, Nate's great-aunt continued. "I am *old*, and *childless*, and very wealthy. I want the best for you. I want *you* to outlive me if nothing else! Is that too much to ask?"

"Of course it isn't. I want to outlive you, too," he said, and instantly regretted how that sounded. "I don't mean that I want you to die, I mean—"

"There's no need to apologize, merely to understand. You feel you *must* help your friend. You *must* see justice done and all wrongs righted."

"Don't you think the same thing?" Nate asked.

"I am old-fashioned, Nathaniel. I hope that one day your wife and family will be happy with you in this house. That you will take your children to the country, chop down a tree, and go home to trim it with them. Read *The Night Before Christmas* to them."

"I don't think any of that ever crossed my mind," Nate admitted.

"I know," Aunt Alice said, stopping in the doorway to admire her niece knotting a ribbon bow. "Thank heavens for girls. So much more sensible than boys."

"Hoo-ray! Nate's here," Allie cried. She ran across the room and grabbed him around the waist, burying her head in his chest. "Isn't this the greatest thing ever?" she asked.

Aunt Alice smiled tenderly toward Nate. Allie loosened her hold on him so she could look them both in the eye.

"I never had kin I got to spend time with. Except my pa, that is. And now I've got an aunt, and a cousin, I think—Deborah, who is entirely so nice. But best of all is having a cousin my age. Nate is just like a brother already."

"Isn't it wonderful?" Nate's mother asked as she entered the room. "Is it a lot to . . . to get used to, Nate?"

"What part of 'it'?"

"Oh, having a cousin. A cousin who's likely to live with us from now on," Nate's mother said.

"Oh, that. I like it," he said sincerely.

Having an interesting, funny kind of kid around who will keep Aunt Alice out of my hair? What could be better?

"Nathaniel, Cook had a tree delivered to the kitchen," Aunt Alice said. "Help her and her daughter stand it up in the corner."

"Oh, can't me and Nate do it, Auntie? I never had a tree with Pa," Allie said.

"Why not?" Nate said. Launching into "Joy to the World" at the top of her lungs, Allie grabbed his arm and pulled him toward the kitchen door.

Bea provided some of the muscle Nate and Allie needed to get the handsome pine tree secured in a stand near the parlor windows. Deborah Fuller made a mountain of popcorn, which "the ladies" strung together with berries and nuts. That was the limit of decorating Aunt Alice would allow. She had been brought up thinking that Christmas trees were every bit as pagan as Norse gods, mistletoe, and Yule logs. Years earlier, it had taken a good bit of arguing by Nate's mother to get a tree in the house in the first place.

"Next year, we will add ornaments," Deborah Fuller whispered to Nate. "She nearly caved in yesterday when Allie said they would look nice."

After dining, the family returned to the parlor. To Allie's gleeful surprise, colorful gift-wrapped boxes were arrayed under the tree.

"Presents!" she shrieked.

"It appears that Saint Nicholas sneaked in while we were eating," Deborah Fuller said.

More likely Marina, thought Nate. *Quietly, too.*

"This one's for me! And this one . . . and this one, too. I can hardly believe it," Allie exclaimed.

"I think it's high time you open one of them, child. You, too, Nephew," said Aunt Alice.

"I'm not ready for that yet," Nate said, rushing toward the hallway. Bea had placed his presents for Aunt Alice and his mother under the tree but had no idea there were more hidden in the sideboard.

"There, *now* I'm ready," he said, adding three packages to the ample pile already there.

"How many presents have you gotten for us, Nate?" asked his mother. "How extravagant."

"Actually"—Nate hesitated—"these three are for Allie. I guess I went overboard a bit."

"You did, assuredly," Aunt Alice added grumpily.

"Godfrey Daniel!" Allie screamed gleefully and proceeded to bear-hug Nate, his mother, and finally Aunt Alice. "I am the luckiest, happiest girl in the world."

"I will not stay up all night for this folderol. Open a present this instant," ordered Aunt Alice. "Both of you."

Nate got the usual, practical presents—a cable-knit woolen sweater, new winter underwear. He thought that one package from Aunt Alice had to be a book with inspirational thoughts appropriate to his age. He was shocked to find instead a copy of *Professional Criminals of America* by the former New York police inspector Thomas Byrnes.

He thanked the elderly woman and asked, "Whatever made you think of this?"

"I may question your activities, Nephew, but I am not oblivious to the way you spend your time. Our minister said this will describe the types of people you should avoid at all cost."

Allie, who had probably gotten enough new clothes to last the winter, was showered with girly presents such as a comb-and-brush set and all sorts of devices to stick into her hair to pin it up or tie it off. And a doll that she loved at first sight. She claimed to love her Puppy Pippin just as much, but Nate knew it wasn't true because the doll never left her hands for a moment. The emerald-colored brooch was a big hit. Allie couldn't stop admiring it after Nate's mother pinned it to her dress.

But after Nate's mother and Aunt Alice had received their presents, one package remained under the tree.

"Silly, ain't you going to even look at what I got you?" Allie asked.

"You bought *me* something?" Nate asked, and Allie bobbed her head in the affirmative. Nate ripped open the wrapping and was shocked. She had gotten him a book called *Houdini's Secrets Revealed* by Osgood Hubbard. The cover promised that the reader—with very little effort and within a matter of days—could become the equal of Houdini. Fame and fortune awaited the reader ready to follow Osgood Hubbard's plan.

Nate was touched by Allie's thoughtfulness, although he couldn't bring himself to crack open the cover. Even if this quack had discovered Houdini's secrets, nobody could become another Houdini overnight! Escaping from a straitjacket while hanging upside down off a skyscraper wasn't something anyone could learn from a book. Neither was escaping from a nailed-shut packing crate thrown into the ocean—while you were handcuffed and leg-shackled.

"I told Allie she found the perfect present for you," his mother sweetly said. Nate nodded and said, "Yes, it really is *something*. Thank you, Allie."

From the pleased look on her face, Nate was pretty certain he had fooled her.

Marina brought cocoa and cookies at that moment, and no more needed to be said. They spent several pleasant hours listening to Aunt Alice reminisce about her younger days. She had been close to her half brother, Jack, before he was banished.

Allie had fallen asleep so soundly that Nate, accompanied by his mother, carried her up the two flights to her temporary bedroom on the servants' floor.

After pushing open the door, Nate's mother fumbled until she found a switch to turn on the single naked bulb allotted to the room. Nate lowered Allie onto the bed, unlaced her new ankle boots, and eased them off. While his mother got Allie ready for bed and tucked her in, Nate found an extra blanket in a hall closet.

Allie woke as he draped it over her. "Nate, I bet your friend Houdini will be real impressed when you learn some of his tricks."

"I expect so," he said, closing the door after turning out the light. Then he pushed it open again and asked, "Would you like to see him perform sometime?"

"Of course I would, silly."

"I'll try to arrange it." Before closing the door again, he added, "You don't need any more excitement for a while."

"So I'll go with you and him next time."

"Go to sleep," he said, avoiding promises he didn't want to make.

Thanks to Aunt Alice, he had nothing to worry about on that score. They spent Christmas Day the way his great-aunt prescribed: church in the morning, a holiday meal in the afternoon, Bible and inspirational readings in the evening.

Allie happily went to bed early, in the company of her dolls, without a single mention of Houdini.

20

It was back to the case the morning after Christmas. Houdini arrived in a taxicab to collect Nate. Soon the duo were speeding back to the Bowery, as planned.

"Will I never have the pleasure of an introduction to your cousin?" Houdini asked. "I understand that she is quite a character."

"Not today, that's for sure. Aunt Alice and my mother have plans for her. And they *specifically* listed places that are off-limits to her, starting with the Tombs, police stations, and the entire Lower East Side."

"Quite comprehensive."

"Aunt Alice said she was certain to think of more," Nate said, not mentioning that the Houdini workshop was one of the forbidden destinations. "How do you know about Allie anyway?"

"My ever-considerate wife has had several telephone conversations with your mother about Ace's predicament *and* your involvement. The youngster's recent arrival came up quite naturally."

"That explains why Aunt Alice is always so calm with me. She hears everything from my mother and blows up at her."

"Saints visiting on earth, that's what mothers are," Houdini whispered, staring out the grimy taxi window. "Speaking of saints, Detective Goodwin spent Christmas Day making inquiries."

"Did she develop any leads?"

"A few villains in Crazy Butch's crew hinted that Ace's arrest might be a warning."

"What sort of warning?" Nate asked.

"Along the lines of 'It's for life when you join a gang, and if you think that's not true, look what happened to Ace Winchell.' "

"Butch admitted that Ace would never have been arrested if he still belonged to the gang," Nate said. "Settling the score makes a lot of sense—especially now that we know Butch was in love with Ace's mother."

"Butch waited all this time? How patient. But what is the family debt? Who owes it?" Houdini asked nobody in particular while impatiently rapping the window with his fingertips.

Before Nate could offer a speculation about the family

debt, the entertainer changed the topic. "Detective Good-win noticed that the wording her informants used was so consistent, it sounded as if they had memorized a script."

"You think Butch put the rumor out himself?" Nate asked.

"To keep his troops in line?"

"Why not? Do nothing criminal and get the benefit of somebody else's evil handiwork."

"Are you excluding Crazy Butch from a role in the crime of the century?" Houdini asked.

"Without hard evidence?" Nate asked incredulously. "I'm speculating, hypothesizing."

"Good," Houdini said with a smile.

"Are we meeting Detective Goodwin somewhere?"

"No, that's not in the cards. I received this message last night." Houdini handed it over.

Mr. Houdini,
Spitting William has "valuable information regard-ing the Slasher kid." Photograph enclosed. Call for William's pedigree, if needed.

Yours,
Detective Isabella Goodwin, NYPD

"Yes, I've already called," Houdini said, answering the first question that came to Nate's mind. "Detective Goodwin tells me that Spitting William acquired his alias at the tender age of twelve."

"What does he spit?"

"Tobacco juice."

"Lots of people chew tobacco and spit the juice. What makes this guy so unusual?"

"Spitting was his weapon of choice when he was a young street thief. His aim was so accurate that from several paces away he could spit a wad of tobacco juice squarely into a man's eyes and incapacitate him. While the victim tried to rub away the foul, stinging liquid, Spitting William would then move in and lift billfold, watch, and any jewelry available."

"But he was caught, right? How else would we know his alias?" Nate said.

"He's been arrested a few times. He progressed into a genuine villain—expert with knife and gun. But he never could shake the nickname among his peers, so he still uses it as a badge of distinction. Spit, which is what Detective Goodwin said to call him, is second in command to Louie the Lump."

"Just like Crazy Butch was second to Max Eastman when Ace was still in the gang."

"Quite so. Spit works for Crazy Butch's rival and is eager to talk about Ace."

"This could be our big break," Nate said hopefully.

Houdini seemed about to say something. Instead, he whistled an old music hall tune until the taxi arrived at Spitting William's place of business.

BRUTAL MURDER ON EAST 54TH STREET

21

The Hell Hole's name was well deserved. Reeking of alcohol, sweat, urine, and smells Nate couldn't identify, the air was sickening. He nearly gagged on it.

The atmosphere obviously didn't bother the saloon's patrons. No small number—men and women alike—were jammed inside, drinking and smoking, laughing and shouting. Many seemed only a short step away from oblivion.

According to a sign above a table opposite the long bar, a "free lunch" was being offered, but nobody was eating. Nate saw why: The meat was green, the cheese was moldy blue, and the bread was infested with crawling animals. The walls were covered with dozens of other signs to amuse the customers. They advised that "The clock is never right" and "If you don't see what you want here, go somewhere and steal it." Nate's favorite was "Play with the cockroaches all you want, but don't take them home with you."

This place is an incubator of all sorts of vermin, he thought as his breathing became easier. *I could learn more about criminals in a day here than in a month of reading.*

Houdini scanned the dark, smoky cavern for the face in the police photograph. He spotted Spitting William at a crowded table near the back of the room.

"Everybody beat it," the man said when Houdini and Nate reached his table. Nate decided that William's companions must have been lesser gang members, because they picked up their drinks and cigarettes and scattered without hesitation.

"Spit's the name," the gangster said, standing and offering a hand in friendship. *Tall, gaunt, sallow-skinned, and stooped.* Nate memorized his features to write down later in his case notes. *Like a character who peeks out from behind the curtains in a spooky house.*

Houdini declined the offer of drinks and asked Spit what interest he had in the case.

"I'm a student of the human race, Mr. Houdini. Have been since I was a boy," their host said. "You can't just walk up to the first citizen you see, spit a walnut-size glob of tobacco juice in his face, pick his bones, and expect to get away scot-free."

"I appreciate the delicacy required," Houdini said appreciatively.

The illusionist is buttering him up, Nate thought, knowing that Houdini's sleight-of-hand abilities were so extraordinary that he could have picked every pocket in the place on his way to this table.

"You gotta look him in the eye," Spit continued, "to know if he's gonna roll over dead or if he's gonna tackle you and scream bloody murder."

"You understand human nature well enough to pick the prime target out of a crowd," Houdini interpreted.

"I did. I still do. But take my friend from boy to man, Butch McGurk. He never could read people."

"You and Crazy Butch have been friends that long?" Nate asked.

"*Was* friends. Being in business with Butch's biggest competitor has made friendship . . . impractical. You see, the Lump and I own this sweet little gold mine—a fifty-fifty split. It's Lump's way of spitting in Butch's eye, you might say." Spit chuckled, which provoked a number of coughs he silenced with a drink from his whiskey glass.

"Louie has some sense of humor. The Lump owns a bar on Houston Street with Kid Twist's little brother. You can imagine how happy *that* makes the Kid."

"Simply fascinating," Houdini said with a huge yawn.

"I get your drift. Enough about me," Spit said. "So here's the thing about your pal Ace. I got a hard time believing that a kid who goes straight for years, and works for a millionaire like you, gets so hard up for seven bucks he flashes the hottest goods in the city."

"The police and the D.A. are the only people who *don't* have a hard time believing that," Nate griped in agreement.

"So being dubious makes me think. I know that Butch holds a grudge for a long, long time—"

"A grudge against Ace for quitting the gang?" Nate asked.

"Kid, he's got a grudge for everyone in that Winchell family that's out of diapers." Spit grinned through brown-stained teeth. "First, *she* drops Butch for that worthless Bugsy Winchell. But Butch forgives all, eventually, and takes Bugsy into the gang. Gives Bugsy a sweet job—good money."

"Didn't he run off and leave the family penniless?" Nate asked, remembering Ace's version of his family history.

"Yes, but didn't Bugsy first steal a fistful of *Mad Max Eastman's* money before he run off?" Spit clarified. "And then—when Butch couldn't find Bugsy—didn't Butch have to make good on the dough?"

"I suppose that made Crazy Butch look rather foolish in the neighborhood," Houdini said thoughtfully.

"Would have ruined him if anybody knew," Spit replied.

"Then how do you know, Mr. Spit?" Nate asked meekly.

"It's enough that I know."

"Untrue," Houdini told him. "Useless gossip."

Spit looked around the bar to make certain their conversation wasn't being overheard and began again in a near whisper. "Maybe Mad Max gets too drunk one night, and maybe he lets the story slip to my boss, Louie the Lump . . .

". . . and maybe Louie told me because he thought it was a funny story. You want to ask Louie about it?"

"So, very few people know that Bugsy Winchell betrayed Crazy Butch before running away?" Nate asked.

"That's right, kid. You want to post a sign or put it in the papers?"

"No, this is most helpful. We understand the sensitive nature of what you have told us," Houdini said. "Did your remembering embrace any other topics that might be of interest to us?"

"Strange enough, it did. I remembered that a string of 'high-society' burglaries happened before the one that got out of control at that mug Cramer's crib."

"You think they're all related," Nate asked, "even though the modus operandi changed so dramatically?"

"Modus what?" Spit asked.

"Excuse our young Latin scholar," Houdini said with a sly wink at Nate. "He means that all the recent mansion burglaries seem identical in style, except for the Cramer case."

"*That's* right, they were," Spit confirmed. "Now then, I

know a good second-story artist. Recently, he's only cracking houses owned by rich, *single* gents—bachelors or widowers. And he always went on nights when the owner *and* the help was away, see? Butler's-night-out kind of break-ins."

"Your burglar friend must get excellent inside information," Nate said.

"Don't go putting me in this. I just know people who know people," Spit insisted. "People say that a mug named Beans Malloy did all the break-ins."

"Including the Cramer job?" Houdini asked.

"If he did the first five or six, it makes sense he did them all."

"Then it makes sense that this Beans Malloy killed Mr. Cramer," Nate asserted.

"No, it doesn't. I've knew Beans since he was a nit, see? He's never done murder. It's not in him. He used to eat beans because he thought butchers' meat was from horses that keeled over in the street—couldn't stand the thought of eating something he'd seen walking around."

Spit laughed at the thought; the laugh quickly turned into another coughing spasm.

"The thing is, he was right. Most of the meat we got was from horses that were on the street that day, makin' deliveries till they dropped."

"So," Nate said, "You, Butch, *and* Beans were best friends as children."

"That's the nail on the head, that is. A teacher called us the Three Musketeers, whoever they were."

"Of course, Beans can't work alone today. He pays protection to Crazy Butch," Houdini said.

"You know your stuff."

"Say, isn't it against your code to squeal on a fellow gangster?" Nate asked.

"You must read too much, kid. Don't you know that's bad for you?" Spit said. "Look, the Italian mob in Greenwich Village and the Chinese downtown, they have their secret codes and all that. Still, they kill each other for a nickel. That's why us Bowery gangs are getting squeezed, see? We're too *nice*."

"If you're *so* nice, why are you ratting out old friends?" Nate asked, trying to push just hard enough.

"They both did me dirt. And more than once. Look, I don't give a rap who did that murder—or who fries for it. But I do have a sweet little business here, see? And I owe that to my partner, the Lump, see? Well, it happens that Louie would very much like to see Butch sizzle. See?"

"Getting one rival out of the way?" Nate asked.

"With Crazy Butch gone, the Lump could dispose of Kid Twist once and for all," Spitting William said, brushing his empty hands together.

"So, giving up old friends is simply . . . a business decision?" Houdini asked.

"I ask you—what isn't?"

22

That gives Butch a double motive for framing Ace—getting even with him *and* with his father," Nate suggested after they reached the relative privacy of the always-crowded avenue called the Bowery.

"Or it could make Butch the patsy in a second frame-up," Houdini said.

"That thought had crossed my mind," Nate admitted. "I guess we shouldn't completely believe anything Spitting William said."

"Certainly not without cross-checking. We need to hear Beans Malloy's side of the story."

Houdini's decision prompted a brisk walk to Detective Goodwin's office in the recently opened Police Headquarters building on Centre Street. Nate wondered if it was a coincidence that it was built at the outside edge of the Lower East Side neighborhood, as was the Tombs five blocks south.

"I had Beans Malloy fitted out for those Fifth Avenue burglaries. That is, until the D.A. laid it all on your friend Ace.

"But I can't help thinking," the detective continued, "that *if* someone like Beans Malloy, a well-known second-story man, was behind all these burglaries . . . well, I see a connection between Malloy and Honest Bill Gates."

"Gates!" Nate said excitedly, remembering his enemy from the used-clothing store. "I just knew it!"

"There's nothing here I can prove, let alone even poke a stick at," Detective Goodwin cautioned, "but most people believe Gates fences the kind of high-end merchandise that Malloy steals."

"Can you pursue that line?" Houdini asked.

"No, not unless I want to be out of work," she answered.

"They'd fire you for solving the case?" Nate asked.

"Truth and ambition mix like oil and water. Our D.A. wants to be governor. Convicting your pal of a string of burglaries and a gory murder is his ticket to the state capital."

"Putting another burglar in the picture complicates it too much?" Houdini asked.

"Exactly. You gents are still on your own, conducting private inquiries," the detective said.

"At least you can point us toward Beans Malloy," Nate said.

"I wish I could. I've been keeping tabs on Malloy since the second Fifth Avenue burglary—hoping he would slip up. But the funniest thing happened—"

"Let me guess. He's dropped out of sight," Houdini said.

"Correct. Nobody's seen Beans since the night that Cramer was murdered."

Nate and Houdini turned toward each other, deep in thought until Nate suggested bouncing these latest revelations off their imprisoned friend. An hour later, they all met around a table in an interrogation room at the Tombs.

"I don't see how I'm ever going to pay you back, Houdini. Ma said you gave her—"

"Silence! Please!" Houdini commanded while grabbing Ace's manacled hands. "Lay-dees and Gen-tell-men, behold!"

The escape artist lifted his right hand to reveal open handcuffs. Ace was free.

"Oh, sir, I wish you wouldn't," the detective said.

"No one can see. And I did no harm to the cuffs."

"You can be a devil," she said as Houdini dove under the table. Ace flexed his fingers and then rubbed his wrists appreciatively.

"Captain Root said it's a good thing you're an honest man, or we'd have had to shoot you years ago. Seeing that you can't be kept locked up."

Houdini popped out from under the table with the padlock that had held Ace's leg-irons shut. "Had I been born of different parentage, I could have developed into a very dangerous criminal," he admitted.

"The *most* dangerous," Nate corrected.

"That's neither here nor there. Ace, let me bring you up-to-date," Houdini said, and proceeded to tell Ace most of what he and Nate had learned since their last meeting.

Ace was simply astounded.

"I've heard of Spitting William—he's a legend," he told them. "But I never laid eyes on him. He was poison to Butch even back then. And I knew Beans Malloy back then, sure. But he couldn't be the Fifth Avenue Slasher. It's not possible."

"Could Butch have done it? Gone along as Beans's accomplice and done the butchery to get at you?" Nate asked.

Ace thought long and hard, and then shook his head in the negative. "No! Butch does have a bad temper. He would do murder without a second thought. But all to get at me? Why should he care so much about *me*?"

"It's not just about you. He wanted to get even with your father, too," Nate said.

"My old man? What does that louse have to do with anything?"

Houdini explained in a low, measured tone.

"I never heard such a thing," Ace said in disbelief. "You sure?"

"It seems likely that your father did steal a large sum—that Butch had to repay—and then went on the lam," Houdini said.

"He was worse than we ever thought. The bum ran out on us with a fortune in his pocket? Gawd, if I could get my hands on *him*, I'd kill him for sure."

Ace's deadly seriousness seemed to alarm Detective Goodwin, who then insisted it was time he return to his cell. Houdini reached out for Ace's hands again, this time applying the handcuffs.

"I feel certain you will never meet again, not after so many years. Put the thought past you," he said. "And I would not share it with your family; it will only cause needless pain."

Ace meekly agreed, still reeling from the thoughts Houdini's revelation had prompted. Nate wanted to volunteer to repadlock Ace's legs—it would have been polite—but couldn't force himself to make the offer. Houdini effortlessly dropped to his knees and clanked the chains shut.

The last thing said as a guard returned Ace to his cell was Nate's upbeat prediction: "It will all be over soon. We promise."

Houdini dropped back into his chair, absorbed in his

own thoughts. He was probably not aware that he had materialized a huge, foreign-looking gold piece from thin air. Or that he was rolling the piece back and forth through his constantly moving fingers. Detective Goodwin was clearly uncomfortable, but Nate's reassuring smile implied that he had seen this before—many times, in fact. Several minutes passed before Houdini smacked the tabletop with the coin's edge.

"Does what we've uncovered square with your impression of Crazy Butch?" he finally asked Detective Goodwin.

"The good or the bad?"

"Both," Houdini said, and laughed.

"Well, I know for a fact that he's generous to some. And I know he's dropped bodies all over the Lower East Side," she said thoughtfully.

"And he wishes one of them was Ace's father," Nate suggested.

"No question there."

"And you think that he was setting up the burglaries for Beans Malloy, giving him the locations and times?" Houdini asked.

"That, and taking the lion's share for his trouble."

"Couldn't Crazy Butch have been Beans's accomplice that night?" Nate asked.

"No. Ace is right. Not even if he thought the crown jewels of Europe were in that apartment."

"You're so certain?" Houdini asked.

"Butch likes being a boss. He doesn't like taking risks since he became a boss," she said.

"That's right. He makes Iris carry his gun," Nate confirmed.

"I fear Beans Malloy is the only person who can really shed light on this," Houdini said after some thought.

"Wait!" Nate interrupted, searching through case notes he had transcribed from memory. "These are roughly Butch's own words: 'I'll swear to you on a stack of Bibles or on my mother's grave—whatever you like. I never saw that cigar case. I got nothing to do with it. If Honest Bill says Ace sold it to him, Bill's telling the truth.' "

"Logic tells us that Honest Bill is lying because he contradicts Ace, and Ace is telling the truth," Houdini said.

"Doesn't the same logic tell us that Crazy Butch is lying, too?" Nate asked. "That they are in it together?"

"Yes, I believe that Honest Bill and Crazy Butch are working together, but they didn't start out to frame Ace— it was simply an opportunity that Butch couldn't pass up," Houdini agreed. "They framed Ace to protect an unknown third person—a sadistic killer."

"There are dozens of Bowery bad guys that Crazy Butch and Gates could be helping out," the detective said.

"But charity always begins at home," Nate said.

23

After Detective Goodwin promised to do her utmost—unofficially, of course—to find Beans Malloy, Houdini and Nate took a taxi homeward.

"Malloy is the key, isn't he?" Nate asked.

"So it would seem," Houdini replied quietly.

"Malloy did all the burglaries, but he brought along an accomplice. A crazy man who tortured and killed Mr. Cramer."

"Calling him a deranged man might be better. A criminally insane person," Houdini said.

"And Gates is that criminally insane person," Nate asserted.

"That is one conclusion too far, my friend. We have no credible proof."

"All we need is Malloy to tell us," Nate said.

"If Malloy, frightened out of his wits, did not board a train to California or a steamer to Europe or South America . . ."

Suddenly Nate realized that they might be much further from a conclusion of the case than he hoped.

"I will call the instant I have anything new to report," Houdini said as the cab moved away from Nate's front door.

As Nate approached, the door opened inward to reveal Allie dressed to the nines: boots so highly polished they could not yet have seen the pavement and a satiny, emerald green dress. Unfortunately, her expression was more forlorn than Ace's had been when he trudged away in chains. Nate instantly felt guilty for ditching her earlier.

"I forgot, I really did," he declared.

Allie said nothing, tears glistening on her cheeks.

"Really, I forgot. Houdini would love to meet you. I'll make up for this. Maybe he'll come and have tea with you. Even show you a trick," Nate promised.

"Will you take me with you next time?"

"That just wouldn't be right. Women can't be detectives." As soon as he said it, Detective Goodwin wagged an accusing finger in his mind's eye. He went on, "Women *can* be detectives, I guess. But not girls. You're just too young to be involved with this . . . mess."

"I'm not scared," she said.

"You would have been scared if you had seen the places we were in today," Nate insisted.

"You think I just fell off a turnip truck?" she asked angrily. "I've seen some pretty scary places."

"I wish to hear all about those places, young lady," said Aunt Alice from the parlor in an unmistakably annoyed tone. "For now, Nathaniel, join me?"

Allie trudged off as Nate prepared for another interrogation by his aunt. He closed the French doors at her request and took a seat on the sofa.

"Allie sure looks swell in the clothes you bought her," he observed.

"Please refrain from using vulgarisms such as 'swell.' A reporter from the *Sun* wishes an interview with you. A reporter from the *Telegram* wishes to interview *me*."

"I suppose that was inevitable," Nate admitted.

"Inevitable only if . . . Oh, there is no point in regretting what has already happened," she said, more to herself than Nate. "Is there any way you can disengage yourself from this investigation?"

"Not while Ace is facing a murder trial and we are closing in on the real culprit."

"Nathaniel, I could order you," she threatened.

Nate stood his ground, saying nothing.

"I could order you just the way my father ordered my brother. That would be unbelievably foolish, wouldn't it?"

"And you're never foolish, Aunt Alice. You really aren't."

The elderly woman's starch wilted. She dropped into her favorite chair and sighed deeply.

"Your father was a born flatterer, too. Have I ever told you that?"

"No, you haven't."

"Reporters snooping into our affairs will certainly shorten my life down to a worthless nub, Nathaniel. I will not order you. But don't you have it in your heart to give an old woman her way?"

"Aunt Alice, I can't abandon the investigation—a terrible injustice is happening." He gave a summary of the case before she could interrupt and finished with a question: "You don't really want me to stop?"

"I've already told you my wishes."

Nate tried to consider his great-aunt's point of view, but his mind kept returning to Ace and his needy family.

"He's my friend," Nate said with great feeling.

"And you think it would be dishonorable to abandon a friend in need."

"That's right."

She sighed and shook her head as if giving up a hopeless cause. "Credit an old lady with having *some* sense. I am wise enough to understand you. You will not bend to my will any more easily than my brother bent to his father's will."

"Thank you, Aunt Alice." Nate walked across the room and kissed her forehead, something he rarely did.

"Get washed and dressed for dinner, Nephew. And ask Allie to come in if you can find her." As Nate turned the doorknob, the unmistakable sound of glass shattering made him hit the floor.

24

Pivoting on one knee, Nate saw Aunt Alice shaking in her chair, fear on her face. The lace daytime curtains had let some broken glass fragments through to the middle of the floor, but most fell harmlessly under the Christmas tree.

A brick had landed several feet away from her. Twine had been wrapped around it several times and knotted— to hold down the piece of paper that peeked out from beneath.

Marina charged bravely in from the kitchen, a rolling pin in hand, as Nate ran to the window, glass crunching underfoot. He looked in both directions and caught a glimpse of a person hurrying away. Nate thought he saw a shock of fiery red hair under a hat as the figure passed under the light of a streetlamp.

Bill Gates? The son? I can't say for sure.

Nate's mother arrived and rushed to comfort Aunt Alice. She delicately picked glass shards from the shocked woman's clothing. Marina stood firm and kept watch, like the Statue of Liberty with a rolling pin instead of a torch.

Nate picked up the brick and began to unknot the twine covering the paper. He was careful to grasp the paper only at the edge until he laid it flat on a side table and read it:

If you and Houdini don't lay off, somebody will get hurt.

You don't want to see your mother as dead as Houdini's, do you?

"What does it say?" Nate's mother asked.

"Just jabber!" Nate said. "I bet it was thrown through the wrong window . . . It wasn't meant for us at all."

"I think you and I should go upstairs," Nate's mother told Aunt Alice. "Nate will get the police, won't you?"

"I want them guarding this house," Aunt Alice said as she left.

Nate asked Marina and Bea not to clean up before the police arrived, but told them it would be all right to cover the broken window before they all froze.

Nate picked up his crime journal in the hall, carefully

laid the note between several blank pages, and put it out of sight—just in case his mother returned. Then he asked the telephone operator to contact the local precinct. As he waited to be connected, a frightening question hit him like a runaway horse.

Where the devil is Allie?

Reporting the crime and getting the desk sergeant off the line as quickly as possible, Nate ran to search every room on the first floor. He dashed up to Allie's room on the top floor. Empty. She wasn't with Aunt Alice or his mother. She wasn't watching Marina and Bea tack blankets over the broken window.

What if she chased after the brick thrower? If Allie was waiting here—waiting for Aunt Alice to finish with me—she heard the brick crash through the window.

The coat hook that had earlier held a child's red winter coat and floppy, wide-brimmed hat was empty. Sick to his stomach, Nate tested the front door. It was unlocked. He knew that he had locked it earlier.

How could she have been . . . crazy enough to put on her coat and follow him? How could I not have seen her on the sidewalk?

Nate returned to the parlor, hoping his cousin would magically reappear.

"Where is Allie, Nathaniel?" Aunt Alice called from the top of the stairs. "Is she with you?"

"Running around somewhere," he said. "I'll send her up as soon as I see her."

"Somewhere! Where is somewhere?" she asked, walking stiffly down the stairs. "Tell me the truth."

"I think she's missing," Nate said as calmly as possible.

"Missing!"

"I looked everywhere. Her coat and hat are gone. And somebody unlocked the front door."

Aunt Alice stared fixedly at Nate.

"I think she might have been by the front door and she heard the brick and looked outside . . . and followed him."

"No! . . . But she is . . . My stars!" Aunt Alice and Nate searched each other's eyes for an answer until Aunt Alice made a startling request.

"We need Houdini. Beg him to come and bring everyone, anyone, he thinks can help."

25

All right, Alice Skinner, you've stepped in it now. You're gonna hear 'I told you so' and 'What were you thinking of' and 'You got less brains than a bag of wet lint' for a month of Sundays."

The two men who had brought her to this cellar—whatever it was—had been quiet for a long time. The silence was scary.

So, sitting in total, inky darkness for what seemed like hours, Allie kept chattering to herself. She alternated between hoping somebody would hear her and being deathly afraid of the same thing. But when she tired and fell silent, fear rose up her gullet. She talked to hold back her mounting terror.

"It's not too cold here, and you can sleep easy on top of all these smelly rag piles. But how long do you want to stay in a dark, stinky cellar? With no food? You got to figure a way out."

She heard a third man join her two jailers upstairs. And this new man sounded madder than a wet hen. Allie couldn't make out much, but she knew that he was cursing and calling her kidnappers "idiots" and "morons." The angry third man ran out of steam pretty quickly, and all three got to talking more sensibly.

"I don't want this new fella comin' down here," she whispered, so quietly that no one upstairs could possibly hear her. "You just had to show that cocky Nate Fuller that girls make as good detectives as boys, didn't you? Couldn't stand him sayin' you were too young to go along. Of course, you could have just sat him down and told him off instead of getting yourself nabbed by the man who threw the brick."

The third man resumed his shouting abruptly. Then came a crash that sounded like a bottle thrown against a wall. Allie was terrified that the third man would come down after her.

"Why didn't you run when that freckly runt turned and came toward you? What'd you think? He remembered he left something in our parlor and was goin' back for it? You should have run before he laid hands on you, Alice Skinner. Next time you'll know better. That's right, next time."

An unoiled hinge screeched, and a shaft of blinding yellow light appeared at the top of the stairs.

"Oh, please, dear Lord, please let there be a next time," she whispered.

26

"I know it's difficult, ma'am, but your family needs you to be strong," Detective Goodwin told Aunt Alice in the reassuring tone doctors use to make children swallow horrid-tasting medicine. She had just arrived, at Houdini's request, and wanted to lower everyone's emotional temperature. "It's likely that the party who threw that brick abducted your niece—"

"So find him! Get her back!"

"*Assuming* that she was taken. Children do go out sometimes without permission," the detective said, calmly finishing her interrupted thought.

"Allie left *seconds* after the brick came through the window. Obviously, she followed the man who threw it. He's clearly the *real* Fifth Avenue Slasher or she would have been home long ago," Nate said in a rush.

"That murderer has the child?" Aunt Alice said, wavering as if about to faint. Nate's mother rushed to her side.

The parlor was literally filled with uniformed policemen who cocked their ears for the detective's reply. After all, the Slasher was in custody.

"There are grounds for any number of theories," the detective said, dodging the issue. "I think we're getting ahead of ourselves."

"Detective, do you need all these officers?" Houdini asked from the dark corner where he had been silently observing.

Grateful for the suggestion, Detective Goodwin posted one officer in the hallway and ordered the rest back to their regular duties. Nothing remained to be done in the parlor, but none of the officers from the local precinct or those who drove Houdini from the Upper West Side had shown any desire to leave. When the room finally emptied, Houdini excluded all prying ears by closing the French doors.

"Your superiors' theory of the case simply doesn't fit the facts, Detective," Houdini said.

"It's not Ace scaring us off the case," Nate said, referring to the threat delivered through his window. "It's the real Slasher."

"A missing child is horrible, but there's no proof she

has been abducted," Detective Goodwin said. "And I cannot organize a hunt for the Slasher on my authority alone."

"Whose authority do you need?" Aunt Alice demanded.

"Captain Root's, but he's on holiday leave. So the chief then, but he will need permission from the district attorney."

"Nathaniel, prepare to take dictation," Aunt Alice said. "I shall send a telegram to the mayor."

"The mayor's a busy man," Houdini suggested.

"He is never too busy to play bridge with us. Nathaniel, are you ready?"

"We don't have time for telegrams, Aunt Alice. You will have to use the telephone," Nate said.

"Very well," she said heavily. "Deborah, will you assist me?"

"I can do it," Nate offered.

"You and your friends have important work to do, if your mother agrees."

Deborah Fuller nodded toward Nate and mouthed the words "Be careful."

Nate nodded back.

"If your great-aunt fails to reach the mayor, I will make a call or two," Houdini said. "Until then, patience."

"With all the excitement, I forgot to tell you that I have Beans Malloy in a cell downtown," Detective Goodwin said.

"How did you find him so quickly?" Nate asked.

"We didn't. I got a telephone tip telling me the name of a hotel in Brooklyn Heights. And the room number."

"An anonymous tip?" Houdini asked.

"It was. And I didn't take the call."

They lapsed into tense silence, avoiding each other's worried faces until Nate's mother returned. "The mayor wants Detective Goodwin's advice. Please hurry."

Detective Goodwin instinctively straightened up, adjusted her uniform, and strode purposefully, as if she were walking into the mayor's office.

"Do you think Detective Goodwin will convince the mayor? Will she try to convince him?" Nate asked Houdini.

"Take heart, Nate. From what I've observed, the detective sees that there is no case against Ace. And the mayor has no ax to grind."

"I think we should search Honest Bill Gates's store first," Nate said.

"But you didn't see his face, did you?"

"No, but I saw his red hair!"

"And no judge will give us a warrant to search an important man's house in the middle of the night because you saw an unidentified man with red hair on the street," Houdini said.

"The mayor told me to do as I see fit to find Allie," Detective Goodwin said, reentering the room.

"What will that be?" Aunt Alice asked, trailing behind her.

"Sorry, ma'am, I should have talked to you first," the detective said, flushed with excitement from advising the mayor of New York City. "Give me a complete description of your niece, starting with hair, eye color, height, weight, clothes last worn."

"Last," Aunt Alice said in terror.

"Just a turn of phrase, ma'am," the detective said. "Let's start with her hair color. The sooner I get this information, the sooner I can send out teams to search. And every foot patrolman in this city will be looking for her."

"And there is a person in custody who might have invaluable information," Houdini added.

"Invaluable in what way?" Aunt Alice asked.

"We think he knows the real Fifth Avenue Slasher's identity," Nate said.

The elderly woman took it all in and said, "Shouldn't you be rushing to interview . . . or interrogate this person?"

"First things first, ma'am: start with Allie's hair color," Detective Goodwin said calmly. Aunt Alice, Nate, and his mother collaborated on a complete description, which Detective Goodwin repeated to a dispatcher downtown. Then she, Houdini, and Nate drove at breakneck speed back to Police HQ on Centre Street. They needed information to find Allie. They needed to break Beans Malloy quickly, so they concocted a plan during the drafty, noisy car ride.

27

"Don't be scared, sweetie," a woman said from the top of the stairs. Allie was relieved that a woman had opened the door. "I'm coming down now, sweetie, and we're going to have a nice little talk. Is that okay with you?"

Allie thought that anything was better than that wild man coming for her.

"I'm coming down the stairs now. Don't you get any silly ideas about running away."

"Oh, no, ma'am," Allie forced herself to say in a wavering voice. "I'm pleased as punch that you want to visit."

The unknown woman cautiously descended the stairs holding an oil lamp at arm's length. Allie couldn't see the woman's face.

"Bringing you here was a silly, silly idea," the woman said, approaching. "We're leaving now. We'll go someplace real nice."

"Why don't you all just let me go home? I'm all tuckered out," Allie said.

"Well . . . you'll go home, sure. First, we want you to have a treat, to make up for . . . well, you know," the woman said as she offered her free hand to Allie. "You like animals, don't you, sweetie? That's terrif! And you call me Iris, okay, sweetie?"

Near the top of the stairs, Allie could hear the wild man. No longer screaming, his voice was as cold and sharp as a hatchet blade.

"God save me from the likes of you. Idiots! You had no cause to threaten those people. Then you make it worse by snatching a little kid. Couldn't leave well enough alone."

The other two men talked back at the same time, so neither could be understood.

"Shut up!" the angry third man repeated until they did. "Believe me, I'll make you half-wits pay for this . . . making me croak a little kid."

28

"You drag me out of my nice, warm bed. Then you leave me for hours, all so some kid can bother me. I've never been played for a chump like this."

"Shut your trap until you're told to talk," Detective Goodwin snapped at the prisoner. Beans Malloy was feistier than Nate expected from a vegetarian who supposedly cringed at the thought of blood. Nate took a big gulp, cleared his throat, and proceeded with the plan.

"I regret that you've been inconvenienced, Mr. Malloy."

"Well, that's a start, an apology. Call me Beans."

"I will," Nate said. "But the thing is, Beans, the inconvenience is permanent. You won't be outside prison until you're buried—"

"What? What the—?"

"Buried after your execution, that is."

"Go chase yourself, kid. What's all this about?" the prisoner asked, turning toward the detective.

"This is a good time to listen, Beans."

"But the kid is nuts! Gibbering like an ape!"

"What harm can he do you?" Detective Goodwin asked.

"I guess," he said, casting a skeptical eye on Nate.

"I know that you are responsible for the Fifth Avenue burglaries," Nate said coolly, thinking about Houdini's instructions. "Including the Cramer burglary. I also know that you will be electrocuted for the vicious murder of Mr. Cramer, even though you're probably innocent of that particular crime."

"I agree. Beans has no prior record of violence or insanity," Detective Goodwin chimed in.

"That murder was insane, you know it. And I'm not nuts," Beans protested.

"Nonetheless, we *can* prove—"

"Prove what? How?" Beans asked, growing uneasy.

"Prove that you were in Cramer's house and that you participated in his murder," Nate said. "You ask 'how?' That is very interesting."

Nate paused to build tension, a technique he had seen Houdini use onstage and off.

"I have just returned from Europe with several recent scientific advances in criminal detection. I know that the Fifth Avenue Slasher was smart enough to wear gloves because he knows that fingerprints are a dead giveaway. But *you* didn't know that every drop of blood is as unique as a fingerprint. That with the help of a French Plasma-scope, we can identify any drop of Cramer's blood we find on your clothes."

"You can go chase yourself then! I like my chances there ain't a single drop of Cramer's blood on my clothes."

Nate stared intently at his quarry. Of course, he knew that beforehand. All the clothes found in Malloy's hotel room had been purchased since the Cramer burglary. Houdini had devised a misdirection for Nate to work on Malloy, and sure enough, it was working perfectly. Now that Beans had acknowledged the power of one phony invention, how could he deny a second?

"Will you bet that you didn't leave a drop of sweat anywhere?" Nate asked. "Because we found at least three perfectly preserved beads of sweat at the crime scene."

"Sweat? So what?" Malloy challenged confidently.

"Every bead of sweat is as unique as a fingerprint. With the brand-new Italian Sudo-commetior, we can dry a sweat drop we take from you and when it matches the sweat we found at Mr. Cramer's . . . well, away you go," Nate said, thanking St. Paul's Day School for making Latin a required course.

"These things ain't real," Beans said. "Are they?"

"Beans, when you were a kid, would you have thought that moving pictures or automobiles or airplanes were real?" the detective asked.

The uncertain crook tried to stare down his opponents, but it didn't work.

"Did Gates work all the burglaries with you? Or just the last one, that went wrong?" Nate asked.

"Gates? Who's Gates?" Beans asked with a worried edge.

"There's no use denying it. Gates was there—the Plasma-scope and Sudo-commetior will prove it."

"You're stitched up tight, Beans. I don't see why you want to take the rap alone," the detective said.

"Go chase yourself," Beans snapped, drumming the table with his fingers faster and faster. "I'm no stool pigeon. I can take the rap."

"It does not add up," Detective Goodwin said, shaking her head. "He had a great career. He was a criminal craftsman; now he goes down as a straitjacket case."

Something seemed to light up in Beans's head. Letting out a sigh of relief, he leaned back in the chair and wrapped his arm around the back. "You ask me why a man like me would do a crime with a man like Mayor Gates. Well, I didn't. And you can't prove otherwise."

"He doesn't want to help himself," Nate said, standing up and opening the door. "Let's air this room out."

Houdini marched in briskly at that very moment.

"Malloy didn't go?" he asked, to which Nate and Detective Goodwin shook their heads.

"Oh, well. He's a dead man now that young Gates confessed."

"The kid?" Malloy yelled.

"The freckle-faced seventeen-year-old. That's the one. Sold you out one hundred percent in a room down the hall," Houdini replied.

"But he said you were looking at the father, not the kid," Beans protested.

"Beans, you know better than that," the detective said. "Mr. Fuller isn't required to tell you the truth."

"What did that loony fink tell you?" he demanded of Houdini.

"That you forced him to come along—at knifepoint—and that you went into an uncontrollable rage when Cramer caught you. Young Billy said he jumped out the window and wasn't even there when you tortured poor Cramer."

"That's perfect. That's the pot calling the kettle black," Beans grumbled.

"You're saying something different?" Nate asked.

"I'm a second-story man; I don't kill people. I was just nosing around the kitchen for some good liquor. I found some and took a few belts because we were in no hurry. I come back to the library and see that batty Gates kid had bashed Cramer in the head, tied him up, and was carving him him with a stiletto. Made me sick."

"How many jobs had young Gates done with you before that night?" Houdini asked.

"None! That was the first time."

"Why did you take him along?" Nate asked.

"Butch," he answered disgustedly. "Butch said the kid was pestering him about how he hated selling clothes. How he wanted some excitement. But how was I supposed to guess that the kid really wanted to be a butcher?"

"A complete and forthright confession of your actual crimes may still save your life," Houdini said. "Nate, please hand him the summary you've just written down."

Nate put a thumbnail summary of the crime as described by Beans Malloy in front of the man and asked him to sign. After he did, Nate, Houdini, and Detective Goodwin all signed as witnesses. The detective then called for a typewriter to come and take a full confession from Malloy.

"Another confession?" he complained.

"Don't worry. That one is sufficient to keep you in jail for the rest of your natural life—and probably keep you out of the electric chair," Houdini told him. "We'll use this to get a search warrant for the Gates store and upstairs residence."

Slowly, the double cross sank in.

"You don't have young Billy Gates next door."

"In the spirit of truthfulness, no," Houdini said.

"And you don't have a Plasma-scope or . . . or the other thing he said."

"Sudo-commetior. It's sort of Latin for sweat measurer," Nate explained.

"At times your language skills are a godsend," Houdini said. "And now we need a judge."

"We need a judge who will open his door at this time of night," added Detective Goodwin.

"You have the authority of the mayor behind you," Houdini said. "And what judge would like to take responsibility tomorrow for leaving a knife-wielding lunatic loose. Right is on our side. The boy *has* to be taken before he does any more harm."

She agreed and called Captain Root for his advice. Judge Percival Potter, who lived on East Twenty-third Street, was the captain's first choice.

When she telephoned, a servant informed Detective Goodwin that the judge did not accept calls after the dinner hour. With no option in sight, the trio hotfooted it to Detective Goodwin's car and drove to the judge's town house.

They all agreed that, under normal circumstances, they would have had more questions for Beans Malloy, questions only he could answer. Who was the brains behind the high-society burglaries? Where did the inside information come from? Where did all the loot go?

First things first, Nate told himself. *We just have to believe that Allie is . . . still alive.*

"I assure you the judge will not see you this evening," the valet informed Houdini, Nate, and Detective Goodwin when they reached his residence. "Nonetheless, I will convey the urgency of your visit to him."

Nearly thirty minutes passed before the valet returned with the message that Judge Potter would see them shortly.

"I wonder how many phone calls he made before deciding to see us," Detective Goodwin said.

It was another quarter hour before the judge appeared. He scolded the detective for not presenting her evidence during normal business hours, then read, reread, and asked her what Nate thought was a ridiculous number of pointless questions about Beans Malloy's clear-cut, no-nonsense confession.

Nate held his breath to keep from screaming until—at long last—Judge Potter issued an arrest warrant for William Gates, Jr., and a search warrant for the Gates property.

The trio rode back to the Bowery at a reckless speed and in complete silence, as if they all heard time relentlessly ticking away.

29

Honest Bill Gates was belligerent when Detective Good-win showed her warrant—stalling for time. The patrol-men waiting for her arrival forced the door open and fanned out to search the three-story building.

Gates's anger rose a few notches higher when his son was handcuffed. Luckily, a search of the boy's room un-covered damning evidence against him—but there was no trace of Allie.

"All right," Detective Goodwin began, "we have a bill-fold with papers belonging to Carl Templeton Cramer. We have two rings, a diamond stickpin, and . . . may your son rot for this," she said with feeling, "we discovered some-thing that wasn't written about in the newspapers." From behind her back, the detective revealed a jar with cloudy liquid and what looked like a bloody ear.

"The Fifth Avenue Slasher took a trophy—the poor man's *ear*. You can't talk your boy's way out of this."

"Look, none of this has to go further," the father bargained. "I can get promotions for all of you—and put a pretty penny in each of your pockets besides. Just throw all this stuff in the East River, okay?"

"Don't waste your breath, because that isn't happening," Detective Goodwin said. "Your boy's a goner. Do yourself a favor and tell us where the little girl is."

Nate had desperately wanted to ask that as soon as they burst through the door, but Detective Goodwin had drilled him in the car on the need to get hard evidence first.

It was after midnight. Allie had been missing for hours. Honest Bill Gates's next words would tell them if they were even on the right track or just wasting precious time.

"She's right, old man," Houdini said sympathetically. "You can't help your son, but you can help yourself."

Two patrolmen returned from searching the basement.

"No sign of a kid, or a struggle," one policeman reported. "The only thing unusual, maybe, was this hat on a step. Looks brand-new, don't it?"

Nate raced over and grabbed the red, wide-brimmed hat.

"This is Allie's hat! It went missing the same time she did."

He turned and thrust it in Honest Bill's face. "My cousin was wearing this hat when she chased after your son tonight. Where is she?"

"Help yourself, Gates. We know the child was here tonight," Houdini said. "Where is she now?"

Dressed only in a long nightshirt and stockings, the formerly belligerent Mayor of Chrystie Street was demoralized and unsteady but reluctant to talk. Until his wife stepped in.

"Bill, tell them or I will," she threatened.

"Listen to your wife, Mr. Mayor," Detective Goodwin urged. "Otherwise, I'll cuff you both. Do you want your wife locked up, too?"

Gates broke like a rain-swollen river overflowing its banks. "I told Billy that the idea of throwing a brick through the window was mad, but he's been impossible since the day that kid came in here," Gates said, looking at Nate. "I couldn't trust him by himself, not in the mood he was in. So I drove him uptown. I thought it would be harmless enough—"

"It nearly hit my great-aunt," Nate said.

"You can't think straight when your own flesh and blood goes crazy," Gates said in his own defense. "This happened because of those reformers in City Hall. Billy had a good no-show job. He was happy, calm. Then the city fires him. He don't want to sell clothes. He went crazy."

"What about the little girl?" Houdini prodded.

"I saw her following Billy to the car. I pointed behind him—to let him know he was being followed—and the next thing I know is he scoops her up, kicking and screaming, and throws her in the backseat."

"Why didn't you tell your son to let the girl go?" Detective Goodwin asked.

"I did, I did. But he pulled a knife and told me, 'Drive or I'll slit her throat,' so I drove her here. Then we put her in the cellar and . . ."

"And what?" Nate asked.

"And I called Butch. To ask him what to do," Gates said.

"As you called him the night of Cramer's murder," Houdini suggested.

"Yeah, *that* night," Gates said.

"Why did you call Butch that night?" Houdini persisted.

"Because Beans came here frantic. He told me what Billy did, so I called Butch. Butch has always been a friend, and he takes a big cut of my business—he owed me."

"But why pick Ace to frame?"

"That was Butch's idea, I swear. I never even heard of your friend," Gates insisted.

"Why *Ace*?" Nate asked again.

"Butch said he had his reasons, is all. He said, 'Tell the cops it was Ace Winchell.' That was good enough for me. I wanted to save my boy."

"We know Butch's reasons for framing Ace, but why the devil did *you* let your son keep the jewelry and that *physical* evidence?" Detective Goodwin asked.

"I had no idea Billy was keeping an ear in his room," Gates said, sounding truly insulted. "He told me he was so scared of being caught that he threw everything in the river—except the cigar case. He kept it for the cigars and was gonna toss it but forgot to. 'Lucky for him,' Butch said. 'Just what we need to frame a patsy.' "

"What about Allie?" Nate demanded. "Where is she?"

"Butch came around pronto when I called him. Iris came, too. After he bawled me and young Billy out, he said he'd take care of the girl."

"Take care of her how?" the detective asked in a low voice.

"Croak her. Rub her out."

"Did he?" Nate asked, trembling.

"He couldn't. Iris forgot to pack his gat when she got dressed."

"God bless the Sullivan Law," Houdini said.

"Then Butch had a brainstorm. Said he would take the girl to Eastman's pet store—it's only two doors down. Said they'd break in, strangle her with a leash or something, and let Max take the rap."

Nate jumped to his feet and headed for the front door.

"Wait, kid! They never got there," Gates said.

"So what changed?" the detective asked when Nate stopped to listen.

"They walked outside, I was holding the door and Butch was cursing young Billy when, out of the blue, the little girl slams her hand into Butch's backside and he screams like a banshee. Butch lets go of the girl, and she runs away toward the Bowery."

"She slapped him that hard?" Nate asked.

"No, she stabbed him with a hatpin. She waited for the right moment and drove it three inches into Butch's behind," Gates said.

"So she's been out there running—or hiding—for hours?" Nate asked.

"Unless Butch caught up with her, bless her soul."

30

He's gonna kill me the second he finishes killing you, if it makes you feel any better to know," Iris assured Allie.

"Shoot! Somebody will find us sooner or later," Allie insisted.

"Butch will. He's gonna figure out that I double-crossed him. He'll have an army out looking for us at dawn."

"Ah, let him send an army," Allie said. "We'll freeze to death before then."

They huddled even closer together for warmth and giggled, their breath freezing in the air.

"Yeah, let's hope for that. For the record, when I ditched Butch and we came up the fire escape to this roof, I never thought Eastman's roof door would be bolted from the inside. I thought we'd be cozy downstairs until morning."

"It was a good plan, excepting the door being locked," Allie agreed through chattering teeth.

"Why lock it? Who'd want to steal birds anyway? And who'd be crazy enough to steal Mad Max Eastman's cats? Go figure!"

"Iris, when you saw me hiding in that doorway—"

"After you tried to kill Butch?"

"I didn't try to kill him. Shucks, I wouldn't kill a horse-fly."

"I'm just razzin' you, kid, giving you the needle," Iris said, and laughed heartily at her unintended play on words. "Givin' you the needle the way you give one to Butch."

"Come on, Iris. Tell me why you didn't give me up to Butch when you found me. I could hear—he was only just down the block."

"Aah, just be grateful I didn't. What's it matter anyway?"

"It matters," Allie said. "If you told on me, you wouldn't be freezing on this roof. You wouldn't be scared that Butch was going to find us. You wouldn't—"

"All right already. Isn't it enough that I'm here?"

"No, it's not. I want to know," the girl persisted.

"Okay, I wanted a night on the town. Or maybe I'm tired of bein' dragged around by Butch . . . Or maybe I'm nuts. I like that one."

"You're foolin' with me, Iris. You're embarrassed to say you're *not* a hard woman. That's why you forgot to bring Butch's gun. You couldn't be part of doing murder. That's the real reason you helped me," Allie finished with great satisfaction.

"Well, I'd say you are the smartest person I've ever met if it weren't for one little thing," Iris said. "*You're* the reason we're hiding up here."

"I won't make the same mistake next time. Shoot, I never even tried to follow anyone before."

Iris was about to tell Allie it was hardly likely there would be a next time when feet pounding up the stairs panicked her.

31

After sending the Gateses—father and son—to Police Headquarters, Detective Goodwin dispatched two-man search parties carrying oil lamps to look for Butch, Iris, and Allie. The detective, her revolver drawn, led a team with Houdini and Nate.

"Nate, tell us what you know about Allie that might help us locate her," Houdini said as they began a door-by-door canvass of the streets bordering Gates's store.

Nate thought about the cousin he had met only a few days earlier. She was clever. Spunky. Resourceful. Liked to sing and play with electrical appliances. *How could any of that be helpful?* he wondered.

"Nate?" Houdini asked.

"She'll never give up. That's all I know for sure."

"That's a good thought to keep," Detective Goodwin said.

They searched in silence until they found an unlatched door. Houdini shined the oil lamp around the entrance area but saw nothing unusual. As they were leaving, the apartment door nearest the entrance opened a crack.

"Is this going to be all night? The coming and going?" a man's voice asked.

"I'm a police detective." Detective Goodwin held her shield high, approaching the man.

"Women 'tecs now! Then we'll have pigs with wings. And a toilet inside every apartment." He sniggered.

"I assure you, sir, that we are on police business," she said.

"I don't have time for more nonsense," the man said, starting to close his door. Nate bolted forward, quickly enough to block him.

"Have you seen a little blond girl in a bright red coat?"

"And just what is a girl that age doing out on the streets at night? And breaking into this building and hiding from her mother?"

"Her *mother*?" Nate repeated.

"They had a fight—the mother and the girl. The girl didn't want to go home with her mother. What kind of behavior is that? And making so much noise they woke me up in the middle of the night."

"Did you hear their conversation?" Detective Goodwin asked.

"I heard mumble, mumble, but I could tell they were arguing," the tenant said. "By the time I got to the door, they were best friends again—skulked away together like they were playing a game."

Some game, Nate thought, *hiding from Crazy Butch.*

"Did you see which way they 'skulked'?" Detective Goodwin asked.

"That way." He pointed in the direction of Gates's and Eastman's stores.

"You're certain?" Houdini asked.

"I'm not blind, just tired. Now go away before I call for a cop." He slammed the door in their stunned faces, and they stepped back into the street.

"That girl had to be Allie," Nate said.

"The mother could have been Iris," Houdini suggested.

"It would take a lot of nerve to double-cross Butch," Detective Goodwin said. "Risk her life for a stranger? Why?"

"Let's ask Iris when we find her," Houdini said.

Nate tried to square his impression of Iris the vicious killer's gun-toting bundle with the image of her as Allie's protector. That seemed like too big a turnaround to be possible. Except for something else he knew about his cousin.

Allie grows on you quickly.

32

Allie and Iris couldn't move as the man's footsteps reached the roof landing—fear compounded the effects of the cold. They watched the door swing open slowly, and the clear, winter moonlight revealed Crazy Butch's ferocious grin.

"This has been one lousy day, ain't it, Iris?" he said, moving toward them, a long, thin-bladed knife hanging in his hand.

"That's the truth, Butch."

"You going to explain?"

"I don't have nothing to explain."

"You going to beg then?"

"Begging wouldn't do any good with you, would it?" Iris asked.

"Nah, but I'd enjoy it."

"Don't do it," Iris pleaded. "If you kill Allie here, you'll fry for it. Her aunt knows the mayor and governor. You can't get away with killing her. And if you kill me, you can't let her live."

"You have a point," he said, dragging the flat side of the gleaming blade across his chin.

"Why don't you run away, Mr. Butch?" Allie said. "It's an awful big country. You could go to California to make your fortune—just like my pa did."

The gangster's demonic expression cracked; he nearly smiled.

"Cute, kid, that's real cute. The problem is, your 'pa' most likely didn't get sold out by his girl." Butch's angry look returned as he focused on Iris. "You're going to die because nobody crosses Butch McGurk and lives to talk about it."

Butch waved his blade so it glinted in the moonlight and took a step toward Allie and Iris when a distant voice yelled, "Nate, don't!" just as the rooftop door opened again. Nate charged through it. He ran toward Crazy Butch, wielding a broom as if it were a medieval knight's lance. As Butch turned, he took the full force of Nate's charge in his stomach. He landed on his back, screaming with pain.

Houdini arrived next, quickly stepping on Butch's right hand, confiscating the gangster's knife. Detective Goodwin appeared next, winded from charging up three flights of stairs, with gun drawn and handcuffs ready.

"I told you they'd f-find us," a near-frozen Allie chattered.

33

Nephew, my heart may not stand another of these wee-hours explanations," Aunt Alice said.

"Fine with me. I could use some dinner, *and* a late-night snack and then some sleep," Nate replied.

"What? You think I could sleep now? Allie, my child, tell us what happened. And are you warm enough?"

Allie—wrapped in blankets, comforters, and hot-water bottles, and seated near an open fire—was warm enough. She recounted her adventures in detail: being dragged into a car by a red-haired youth, then locked in a smelly basement while people argued overhead, then leaving a clue on the stairs and stabbing Crazy Butch to make her escape.

"How imaginative!" Aunt Alice said admiringly.

"But, Aunt Alice, you're the one who told me that a girl can't ever go too far wrong in the city with a big ol' hatpin handy."

Nate could not remember ever seeing his great-aunt blush before.

"Well, I'm sure that I would never have the courage—or brains—to do half of that," Nate's mother said. Nate, Houdini, and Detective Goodwin then separately congratulated Allie, and she beamed with appreciation.

"There isn't much more to tell . . . about me," Allie said. "I was hiding in a doorway and didn't have the first notion about how to get back here when Iris came along and I went with her."

"Why did you trust her?" Nate asked.

"I guess 'cause of the story my pa used to tell about drowning in a swamp. He always said, if you're drowning and the only thing you can grab on to is a rotten old log full of snakes, grab the log every time."

"Sound advice, indeed!" Houdini said.

"Is anything bad going to happen to Iris now?" Allie asked.

"My stars, no. She's due a reward, if I have any say," Detective Goodwin assured her.

"Where did you and this Iris go then, child?" Aunt Alice asked.

Allie told them how Iris knew where the key to Eastman's Animal Emporium was hidden because she fed all the animals every day while Eastman was in prison. But when they discovered the key was missing and heard Butch in the street, Iris dragged Allie up the fire escape to the roof—because the rooftop door was never locked.

"But tonight it was, and the two of you were trapped," Nate concluded.

"Trapped until you rescued me," Allie said.

"What made you think that Allie would be hiding in the gangster's pet shop?" Nate's mother asked.

"It was more hope than anything else," Nate said.

"It was a most logical deduction, arrived at after a long chain of discovery," Houdini insisted.

"I'm with you on that, sir," Detective Goodwin said. "Nate pegged the son from the beginning. He could have a brilliant career on the force."

"Since Gates's statement implicating Ace was phony," Nate replied, "we knew that he was framing Ace to protect somebody—"

"And charity begins at home, as you wisely pointed out," Houdini added.

"I thought Gates was protecting his son because the son acted so suspiciously. And when I saw a man with red hair outside our parlor window after the brick was thrown, well, it was obvious."

"So you went to Gates's store and searched it?" Nate's mother asked.

"We couldn't do that, not without some hard evidence," Detective Goodwin said.

"But the mayor? Didn't he give you carte blanche?" asked Aunt Alice.

"That he did, ma'am. He also said to watch my step."

"Luckily for all concerned," Houdini said, "everyone played their parts magnificently today. Detective Goodwin tracked down Beans Malloy, the man who actually committed the recent burglaries in this neighborhood. Nate tricked Malloy into confessing to his crimes and revealing that young Gates was the Fifth Avenue Slasher."

"Nate got him to confess?" Nate's mother asked.

"My dear Deborah," Houdini said, "your son exhibits acting genius rarely seen outside London's West End theaters. We devised a plan before interviewing Malloy, a plan acted to a T by Nate."

"We pretended we had brand-new machines that would identify people from their blood or even drops of sweat," Nate said proudly.

"How unpleasant," Aunt Alice said. "Ingenious, but unpleasant."

"Ma'am, if only we had such machines," Detective Goodwin said.

"Someday," Houdini said. "Who knows?"

"Anyway," Nate continued, "it was really easy to fool Malloy and get him to tell us everything we needed."

"But why did my nephew conduct this interview?" Aunt Alice asked with narrowed eyes.

"We thought Detective Goodwin could hardly pretend to have detecting machines at her disposal that Malloy had never heard of," Houdini explained. "It was vital that they had been brought recently to New York—newly invented in Europe."

"Again, sir, why my nephew?"

"Aah! The price of being world-famous," Houdini said. "Malloy would likely have recognized me and suspected that there was hocus-pocus afoot. We had one good shot and very little time—young Allie was in danger—so we decided that Nate had to take it."

"I, for one, am glad my son is using his brains rather than his brawn," Nate's mother said.

"He sure did use his nerve when he ran into that crazy old Butch with a broomstick. He stuck him like a hog," Allie said.

Nate's mother gasped slightly, rose from the sofa, and said, "It's time for bed. I would prefer to hear more tomorrow . . . if hearing more is necessary."

"It's good results for a day's work," Detective Goodwin said. "We caught a dangerous killer, solved a string of burglaries, and bagged a notorious gang leader."

"We still don't know how the burglary operation worked," Nate protested. "Or who provided the inside information."

"Why don't you leave that to us on the force? You've done more than enough for now," the detective said.

"And I believe you still have a few math problems to solve, Nate," his mother said as she and Aunt Alice made for the stairs. "To bed now."

"Oh, but I can't possibly sleep," Allie said, jumping up. She shucked her covers and ran to Houdini, hugging him around the waist.

"I bet I'm the only person in this house . . . why, in the whole of New York City, I bet I'm the only person who hasn't seen you do some wonderful trick or escape or something."

"Allie, you can't ask Houdini to do a trick that way!" Nate insisted.

"What way should I ask?" she replied.

"I think you asked in the most pleasing way I have ever heard, young lady," Houdini said. "Give me a second to think."

Houdini walked to the corner of the room. Nate assumed that the entertainer must be retrieving something from his hidden hanky-panky pocket, and indeed he was.

"Here I have a four-foot length of fine blue silk. Detective Goodwin, take it and pull it. Assure the young lady that it is one, unbroken piece of cloth."

The detective complied, much to Allie's growing delight. Nate watched in amazement.

How many hanky-panky pockets can Houdini have? He never repeats himself.

"Now, Nate, would you find a pair of shears, please?" Houdini continued. Nate quickly found scissors in a sewing basket next to his mother's parlor chair.

"Excellent. Now watch very closely, young lady. As

Detective Goodwin and I each hold one end of the fabric taut, Nate will cut the fabric in half."

Nate did, then Houdini grabbed the uncut end and had Nate repeat the act, cutting the remaining piece in half. They continued in that manner until the piece Houdini and the detective stretched out for Nate was barely large enough to cut. Allie was giddy with excitement.

"Look at the mess we've made here," Houdini tsked. "Detective, may I borrow your cap a moment?"

The detective handed over her blue uniform hat, which Houdini held upside down in his palm. He asked Nate to gather up all the cut fabric and drop it in the hat. Then he walked over to Allie with the hat in his right hand, waved his left hand across the top, and repeated "abracadabra" three times.

"Young lady, my present to you," Houdini said, extending the hat toward Allie. "Reach inside, please."

She did as requested and began slowly pulling out the blue silk—magically rejoined into one piece.

"Oh! Thank you, thank you," she said as Nate and Detective Goodwin applauded in admiration.

"What do you think of that?" Nate asked Allie as she wrapped the silk around her neck.

"I guess . . . I wonder . . . what's going to happen to me next?"